CW00554607

DARK OF NIGHT

EPISODE FOUR

C.S DUFFY

ABOUT THE AUTHOR

C.S. Duffy writes crime thrillers with a healthy dose of black humour. Her background is in film and TV, and she has several projects in development in Sweden and the UK, including the feature film *Guilty*. She is the author of *Life is Swede,* a thriller in the form of a blog - leading several readers to contact Swedish news agencies asking them why they hadn't reported the murder that features in the blog.

www.csduffy.com

f facebook.com/csduffywriter

▼ twitter.com/csduffywriter

◎ instagram.com/csduffywriter

PRAISE FOR C.S DUFFY

I think Glasgow has just found itself a fresh new name in crime fiction! Dark of Night is short and sharp, full of the Glasgow banter and humour laced with a good old-fashioned murder mystery....The characters in the book are authentic "Glesga" characters with that dry wit, irreverent humour and that way of telling a stranger your life story if you stand beside them for longer than 5 minutes, shone throughout the book.
ChapterinMyLife Blog

...For all they are about a serial killer, there is a lot of humour in them too and a real sense of warmth towards Glasgow and its people. CS Duffy has created brilliant and very likeable characters in Ruari and Cara who both feel very authentic in their thoughts and actions.
Portobello Book Blog

Set in Glasgow this is pure Scottish gold. The descriptions of the area sound very authentic to the point I think I could do a tour of the City and Campsies just from my knowledge from the book. Then the characters have that natural interaction that just brings them to life with a raw quick-witted humour.
Books from Dusk Till Dawn

The book is fast paced and the readers are hooked since the beginning. This is the story of a man's obsession to find a serial killer. The story has so many twists and turns that readers won't be able to catch their breath...
Book Worldliness Book Blog

Reader Reviews of Dark of Night

"Couldn't put it down"

"Fast paced Tartan Noir at its best. And OMG what a cliffhanger"

"With twists and turns that will keep your head spinning and a touch of comedy that brings her characters to life, this is one you won't want to put down."

"Seriously invested in the characters and very much enjoying the Glesga banter and humour."

"I read this book in just a few hours and OMG the cliff hanger!"

"Truly loved it!"

"Absolutely love the book, captivating, full of suspense and really funny in bits too."

"Pure gave me the chills."

"I rarely read fiction books but sweet mother this was epic... read it in one go and have been checking daily for episode 2... I can't believe we are being held on that cliffhanger."

"Twists and turns, characters you fall in love with.....and hate! A great read."

"Watch out Brookmyre and MacBride - there's a new author in town who's adding their own splash of colour to Tartan Noir. C.S. Duffy nails it with a funny, engrossing and disturbing tale of love, murder and more in a uniquely Scottish way - I can't wait for the next book."

1

J ade shivered and she wasn't sure if it was from cold or shock. The hills all around her were just murky outlines shrouded in a dull whiteness and the air was wet and icy. She could hardly remember the sensation of being warm.

Her vision was blurry with exhaustion, her muscles so fatigued her movements were jerky and uneven. Every step jolted her aching joints and the swelling of her bruised throat was pressing on her windpipe, making each breath a short gasp of desperation.

This never happened in films.

In films, the heroine escapes the monster and falls directly into the arms of some brawny detective who risked everything in his single-minded determination to save her. She wasn't left to stagger about in the freezing pitch darkness on her own, tripping over wire fences, treading on brambles and nettles and those wee jaggy bastards that were like nettles but spikier.

Heroines almost never have to contend with sheep shit.

At some point in the night, Jade had skidded on a pile of

droppings on a steep verge and ended up tumbling over rocks and stones, pure raging at the thought of having fought off an evil murdering shithead only to be done in by a load of sheep jobbies.

Some time later she found a road. She thought it might be the wee road that cut through the Campsies between Lennoxtown and Fintry, but it was, after all, a narrow strip of tarmac surrounded by grass and sheep and rain: it could literally be anywhere in Scotland. Something about it was familiar, she thought, and a tiny spark of hope ignited in her. It was the road she thought it was.

Jade could remember squealing when she was lifted off the bus seat as it flew merrily over potholes along this road on the way to visit her Granny in Fintry. Not her Gran, her other Granny. She could never remember which one of them you were allowed to shove off a bus, but if she had to chose, it would be the Fintry Granny. She had a wee pinched mouth like a cat's bum and only ever had jammy biscuits in when she knew fine Jade hated jam.

Blood was trickling from somewhere along Jade's hairline. When she wrenched herself from his grasp and scrabbled over the remains of an old wall, she had plunged headlong into the dense foliage on the other side and nutted herself on a rock. She had bitten her lip to stop from screaming when her forehead collided with the jaggy edge of the rock and she could still feel the sharp, metallic taste of blood in her mouth. She had frozen, crouching on the grass behind the wall, certain that at any moment she would feel his icy fingers close around her ankle and yank her back, but they never materialised.

The massive, sheep's bum wool jumper she was wearing was scratchy and sore around her tender neck, but she was grateful for its warmth anyway. She couldn't say much for the past few hours, but the jumper had kept the worst of the hypothermia away, so that was something. For the millionth time, Jade felt for her bag. Then, for the millionth time, she remembered swinging it in his face, feeling the satisfying thud of its weight colliding with his nose as he yowled in pain. He had grabbed hold of the strap and yanked it: she let go and scarpered.

When she first started going out in town, Gran sternly ordered her to always immediately give up her purse if she was mugged. At the time, Jade laughed that the city centre was fine these days. The razor gangs of Gran's youth were all doddery wee old men now, and the good thing about bams off their heads is that they rarely have the coordination or mental wherewithal to do much damage to anybody but themselves. Gran shook her head and insisted again that no purse was worth her life.

She'd been right enough there. Jade was still breathing. She might be beaten and bruised and sore and exhausted and terrified, but she was upright. She'd heal. She would wake up tomorrow morning, refreshed and revived and grateful to be around, and she would make a start on putting her life back together. Dumped one day and nearly murdered the next. She'd had a belter of a weekend.

The roar of an engine disturbed the stillness of the morning. A tiny electric blue hatchback, souped up to within an inch of its life, screeched around a bend in too-low a gear, the deafening bass from some Euro-dance horror thudding through the air. It crossed Jade's mind that she didn't know who was in the car -- maybe she should hide, or duck, but the thought of doing anything other than staggering in a vaguely forwards direction was insurmountably exhausting, so she just carried on until the car pulled up alongside her.

It was rammed, to clown-car proportions, with a shower of Neds. They all appeared to be at that exact stage of teenage growth spurts where their hands and feet seem a bit too big for the rest of them, like puppies, except puppies who would thieve the wedding ring off a corpse. The driver rolled down the window and Jade was hit by an overpowering stench of BO, with base notes of weed and overtones of the sort of cheap cologne that promises to turn women to jelly. In fairness, her knees were weakening, but probably not in such a way that would be of any use to the raging testosterone-fest in the Nedmobile.

The driver, his shaved skull covered in an inexplicable tattoo of a teddy bear grinned, revealing a gold tooth. He was saying something, but Jade couldn't make out the words. Blood rushed in her ears and it sounded as though he were speaking from under water.

There was an angry-looking spot on his chin. He had tried to cover up with a glob of foundation several shades too dark for him, presumably nicked from a severely tanned sister. Jade's heart went out to him and all of a sudden a heaving sob crashed over her like a tidal wave and then she was on the ground, icy dew beneath her ravaged fingers.

'Oh shit — quick, somebody phone the police — missus, missus are you okay? 'Mon now missus, breathe with me, okay? You're okay now, you're safe.'

Jade bent double, kneeling on the grassy verge as though physically holding herself together, empty, aching sobs that were half screams and half gasps for breath wracking through her body. The wee Ned rubbed her back until police sirens approached in the distance.

2

Jade woke up and the relief that she was in her own bed was so great that she nearly started crying all over again. She lay a moment, enjoying the soft familiarity of her own sheets and pillows and the pattern of the shadows on the ceiling from the venetian blinds covering the bedroom window.

Andy hated the blinds. He'd done nothing but moan his face off about them ever since he'd moved in. Jade hadn't actually had particularly strong feelings about window coverings — the blinds had been up when she bought the flat and she'd just never bothered to change them — but regularly insisted they were staying because she found his incessant whining about them a bit unbecoming and frankly weird. Who in their right mind was that passionate about curtains?

Well it was definitely none of his business now, Jade thought, fiercely swallowing back the tears that sprang into her eyes. She could put up blinds in the living room and kitchen too, just for good measure, if she wanted. She might even replace all the doors with blinds, or have them randomly hanging from the ceiling here and there. She would tell people they were an art installation to remind her never again to fall for such a fanny.

Jade burst into tears.

Damnit.

She should get out of bed and have a nice bath, she thought when the sobs finally started to subside. She blew her nose and wiped the tears from her cheeks, determined to pull herself together. Her scalp had been too tender to properly wash her hair when she got home from the hospital, and she had a horrible feeling that she looked even more like the creature from the Black Lagoon than she normally did first thing. Looking a bit more human would help her feel a bit more human. Judging by the pattern the blinds created on the ceiling, it was mid-morning or so, and she was due at the police station at noon.

See Andy? You can't tell time with curtains, can you now, she thought. She wiped her the last of her tears with the back of her hand and fumbled on the bedside table for a pen and her journal.

The truth was, Jade would have liked to have been the sort of person who kept a journal more than she actually was one. It was a fancy hand stitched journal she'd bought from a craft fair in the West End once upon a time and it mostly sat there as decoration, gathering dust. But she had been such a mess when the police tried to talk to her at the hospital that she wanted to try to write down what she could remember so she was better prepared. Then, if that hard, tight feeling filled her throat again when she tried to speak, trapping the words inside, she could at least pass the notes over to the detectives.

It was all a bit of a blur, the hospital. In the ambulance they had given her a jag to calm her down and everything had gone floaty. She remembered waking up on a stretcher in a cubicle surrounded by green curtains, listening to the din of folk in groaning pain, a baby crying, a drunk singing.

What was it about every Glasgow man of a certain age that the minute he got a drink in him he thought he was Sinatra? It had just been her and Gran for most of Jade's childhood, maybe that was why she was unfamiliar with the ways of men of a certain age.

Gran liked a wee drink, but she only sang when she'd had a whisky and that was only on Hogmany. She owned a single bottle of Glengoyne, a special edition someone had given her back at the dawn of time, and once a year she would reverently pour herself a single nip for the Bells. When Jade got her first job, she offered to buy Gran another bottle or two so that she could have a wee dram whenever she liked, but Gran insisted it was much too expensive and to save her money.

For their regular Friday night session, Gran and her best pal and favourite adversary, wee Jeanie from across the hall, favoured some godforsaken alcopop that turned their tongues blue and made them cackle wildly, clutching their sides and swaying like Weeble dolls in tracksuits. On several occasions, Jade tried to explain that there was a long way between a bespoke single malt and a 47 pence concoction of sugar and regret, but Gran just giggled her face off and eventually Jade gave up.

Despite the objections of some distant auntie who had no say in the matter anyway, Jade decided to scatter Gran's ashes over Drumgoyne because she liked the idea of her being free to haunt the distillery and have all the drink she wanted without her tongue turning blue. Unfortunately, she had imagined the romantic notion without accounting for Scottish wind. If there is a worse way to say goodbye to the woman who raised you than coughing and spluttering and blowing her out your nose, Jade would like to know what it was.

At the hospital the night before, the police had tried talking to her at least twice. The first time, she had been too woozy to even focus on their questions and had fallen asleep while they were still talking. The second time, she had started gasping for breath before they could even ask her a question. She been given a paper bag to breathe into.

The detectives had sounded distorted and weirdly distant. They washed over Jade as she curled up on the stretcher breathing into her bag and feeling annoyed at herself for being such a rocket. Just tell them what they need to know and get it over and done with, she told herself sternly. But the words wouldn't come.

The nurse who had stitched up Jade's forehead asked the police if they thought it had been the Dancing Girls killer who attacked Jade. One of the detectives replied that it was unlikely. Alec McAvoy, the mastermind who hadn't murdered anyone but manipulated others to do his dirty work, had been pushed out a window by the sister of one of his victims the night before. The police had just been about to arrest him, but now he was upstairs in the intensive care unit, clinging to life. The sister was being charged with attempted murder. Someone asked if McAvoy was likely to survive.

'Aye, probably,' spat a female voice, laced with bitterness. 'That sort are like cockroaches, aren't they? He'll lie there getting sponge baths til kingdom come. Bastard.'

'Well he's certainly not a danger to anyone any more,' replied a male voice, yawning deeply. 'That's something, at least.'

Jade realised now that her hand was trembling, and she

dropped the pen onto the duvet. She would have her bath first, she decided. Then she would sit down and force herself to remember something that would be helpful for the police.

It was all a nightmarish mosaic of vague impressions. A hand grabbing. Her head snapping back. An inhuman growl. Teeth, nails, icy fingers closing around her throat. Her own wild screech as she somehow twisted free, the sweetness of air rushing into her lungs, the moment of giddiness when she leapt over the wall and left him behind.

Jade got out of bed, and realised that she wasn't nearly as sore as she thought she'd be. 'It's mostly superficial,' the nurse cheerfully announced as she daubed and scraped and sewed. 'You'll have a wee headache in the morning, but you'll be as good as new in no time.' Jade didn't quite have her confidence, but she was relieved to feel halfway human all the same. She would have a quick shower instead of a bath, she decided, and maybe even pop to the gym before she had to be at the police station. A session on the punching bag would make her feel herself again, she thought.

She tripped over something lying on the floor. Andy's jumper. He must have left it in his hurry to pack the other day.

She sank onto the carpet and hugged it to her, breathing it in, desperate for a sense of him. It didn't smell familiar, just a bit musty and old, the scratchy wool making her want to sneeze. It had probably already been lying there for days before he abruptly decided they were over, she thought with a dry chuckle, affection mixing with her tears as she folded it on her lap. Neither of them were exactly what you'd call house proud.

Bugger the gym, she thought resolutely, getting to her

feet. She would take it round to him. He'd given her the address he would be staying at in case she needed to forward post or anything. She should tell him about the attack anyway, she thought. Break up or no, that wasn't the sort of thing he should hear about on the grapevine. And who knew, maybe they would get chatting, and he would realise that the whole break up thing was a stupid idea and he would just come back home where he belonged.

She would even get some curtains for the bedroom.

ANDY DIDN'T LOOK EXACTLY THRILLED to see her. Too late, Jade remembered they had specifically agreed not to contact each other for a few weeks to let the dust settle, and here she was the very next day. Well, he had specifically agreed and she had been too distraught to formulate an argument, but obviously it was a stupid idea. They had lived together for nearly three years, obviously there would be stuff they'd need to discuss, even if he hadn't left his jumper behind.

'I could have thrown it in the bin,' she said with a grin she suspected looked a bit manic. He busied himself getting mugs out and faffing with teabags, refusing to meet her eye, and Jade tried her best not to be stung at how cold he was acting. *Things are bound to be weird to start with*, she reminded herself, determined to ignore the lump forming in her throat. Any minute now one of them would say something daft and they'd laugh and start blethering and feel like them again.

When he'd opened the door, looking so achingly familiar in an old T shirt and joggers, she'd felt such a rush of affection it nearly took her breath away and she couldn't for the life of her remember what they'd ever fought about. He was tall and lanky, his thick mid-brown hair mussed in is usual just-got-an-electric-shock kind of way, and it was an effort not to reach out and fix it for him.

It seemed so bizarre now to think that their similar colouring had put her off the first time she saw him roaring his head off at some goal or other at The Record Factory. Jade and her best pal Hannah had popped down for a quick catch up and were gutted to find it packed with baying football fans and a game droning on the big screen.

"Mon we'll walk up to Ashton Lane,' Hannah had said, wrinkling her nose in disgust as something apparently displeasing occurred on the pitch and a howl of anguish ripped round the bar. 'One of the pubs there should be safe.' But Jade had spotted Andy, and even though she worried that night they looked a bit creepily like brother and sister with matching brown hair and eyes, that was that. Until now.

The kitchen was unexpected, she thought now, watching Andy put the sleek chrome kettle on. It was all space-agey metallic surfaces and fancy gadgets, not to mention disturbingly neat. She thought he had gone to stay with one of his pals from the pub five-a-side team he played on, but they all lived in manky boy-flats.

This kitchen was in the home of a grown up. The mugs matched. A nasty feeling started to prickle at the edge of Jade's consciousness.

'Sorry about the face,' she blurted. The kettle had come to the boil and Andy's back was to her as he poured water into two mugs, but she thought she saw him flinch. 'It looks worse than it is. Hospital said I'd be fine in a few days.'

'Aye, that's good,' muttered Andy, handing her a mug. Jade reminded herself he had no idea what had happened to her. How could he be expected to be worried when he didn't have a clue? He probably just thought she'd nutted herself with the punching bag at the gym. It wouldn't be the first time. She should start telling him what happened, but suddenly it didn't seem to matter.

'Look I know we said about, taking a total break for a wee while and everything,' she blurted, 'I just — I honestly forgot when I saw your jumper. I jumped in a taxi without thinking. I'm sorry, it's just — the last couple of days, it's been a bit of a —'

Shit. Jade could feel tears building. She had promised herself she wouldn't cry in front of him. 'I just feel like it was all awful fast to be calling it a day just like that. I understand you've not been happy, but can we not talk a wee bit, just see if —'

'Listen, Jade, just —'

'What is that?'

Hot chills danced over Jade as she clocked the wee bowl on the counter. It was brightly painted, deep blues and yellows vaguely suggesting a Mediterranean holiday. It was filled with lip balms of all different shades and flavours. Jade was confident none of Andy's five-a-side pals wore lip balm.

'Whose are they?'

'Listen, Jade, just —'

'Who are you staying with Andy?'

'Jade, put your tea down —'

'Are you — are you staying with a woman?' Jade could feel blood rushing in her ears. She hadn't expected this. Whatever she thought was going on with him, it wasn't this.

It couldn't be true. He wouldn't do this. She must have got the wrong end of the stick, somehow. 'Did you — have you been cheating on me?' She didn't like the sound of those words in her mouth.

'Jade, just have a wee sit down and I'll —'

'So you just, what? Just happened to meet somebody

innocently in the past forty-odd hours you've been single and decided not to waste any more time? Fuck's sake, Andy, four years we've been together. Could you not have taken more than half an hour to get over me? Here's me thinking we could still talk, maybe even salvage — and you're already shacking up with some random —'

'Jade, please, sit down a minute, try to think —'

Just then, the front door opened and a woman bustled in, balancing a baby on her hip. Long blond hair and an open, friendly face, she was muttering some lullaby under her breath as the baby mewled irritably, worked its way up to a walloper. Jade stared, stunned.

'Andy I've left the nappy bag in the lift, gonnae —' She caught sight of Jade and her expression darkened. 'Oh, for fuck's sake.'

'Jade —' Andy's voice was distant over the rushing of blood in Jade's ears.

Jade was shaking her head, feeling her hands tremble as confusing, cruel memories darted in and out of her mind, too quickly for her to catch hold of them before they were gone. Andy prised the tea from her hands. The baby started to howl.

'I don't have time for this, no' the day,' the woman snapped, shoogling the baby. 'I'm sorry, it's a terrible shame that your ex-girlfriend is mental but you need to get her oout my house. The wee one needs his nap and I'm not having her cutting about the place, frothing at the mouth. Get her out.'

With that she slammed a bedroom door and the bang reverberated in Jade's ears as she shook her head, numbness seeping through her. She turned slowly to Andy. 'I — I don't — I don't understand —'

'Remember how this happens sometimes,' he said

gently. She felt the warmth of his hand on the small of her back. It was comforting, but it woke up a memory she didn't like so she shook him off. 'We didn't just split up.'

She shook her head again. 'No, it was — it was just — you left your jumper on the floor.'

'That's not my jumper. Look —' Andy gestured to the hallway mirror and Jade stared at it. Her face was fine. No cuts, no bruises, though as the image came into focus and hot pins and needles darted over her, Jade noticed the tiny, faint scar on her temple. She remembered the long-ago sensation of blood dripping down the side of her face, the tightness of her bruised windpipe. His icy fingers closing around her throat.

'It was two years ago.'

IT HAD BEEN 732 days since Stellan disappeared.

It was the first thing DCI Cara Boyle thought when she woke up each morning. The night she had got home after the Alec McAvoy arrest had gone so wrong, she had been surprised when he didn't come to meet her at the door as he normally did when he heard her car crunch up the gravel drive. Sharp unease prickling up her spine, she had rampaged through the house shouting his name, certain that any second she would come across him curled up in the kind of wee nook he liked to read in.

He had a funny habit of finding random places in the house to hang out: the window seat on the first floor landing, the patio swing even in the dead of winter, the battered armchair in the spare room.

Cara had found that old chair at the Barras more than twenty years before and lugged all the way home to her first flat which overlooked the Necropolis. It was faded and threadbare and ugly as sin, but in it Cara had studied, laughed until she cried with girlfriends, sobbed over long-forgotten heartbreaks and once, memorably, sooked spilled wine out of to the cheers of her friends, leading to neverending years of jokes about the luck of any man she dated.

'Haud on tight, pal,' her friend Alan had told then-twenty-one year old Stellan, slapping him on the back and nearly knocking him over. Alan was a huge bear of man who was known in their crowd as Tiimm-berrrr thanks to his habit falling asleep standing up in the middle of dance floors when he'd had a few. He was a gentle giant and the kind of pal who would bury the body for you, no questions asked. He died of lung cancer the year their uni crowd turned thirty, and the nights he had spent sprawled across that armchair, snoring like a pneumatic drill, were one of the reasons Cara couldn't bear to part with it.

'We have a living room, you know,' she'd grinned to Stellan one Saturday, just a few weeks before he went missing. She had been on her way to visit Amy Kerr in prison in the hopes of getting her to finally open up about what she knew about Alec McAvoy, and she couldn't find her favourite long sleeved T shirt. She thought it might be in the to-be-ironed pile that was shoved on the spare room bed, and had found Stellan lounging sideways in the chair, dangling his legs over the armrest, reading.

He'd grinned and pointed out it was more comfortable than the showy Chesterfields they both regretted buying for the living room, and added that it reminded him of her when she was gone. She'd rolled her eyes with a laugh and called him a fanny. She'd been about to dart over and kiss him when she spied the T shirt she had been searching for, and dashed out the door instead.

Cara had spent a lot of time over the past two years counting all the opportunities she had missed to kiss Stellan.

When she finally admitted to herself that night that the house was empty, that he would have been able to hear her shouting for him even with his noise cancelling headphones on, she had sat down on the stairs and called the police. It didn't occur to her to do anything else, but when the lassie who answered the 999 call doubtfully asked if she was sure he hadn't just gone out with pals, she wished she had thought it through more. She backed up and explained that she was a DCI in an attempt to make them take her report seriously, but the dispatcher gently told her that she'd send someone round to 'have a wee chat with her,' and she suspected she hadn't been believed.

Sure enough the pair of constables who showed up looked as though they shouldn't be out on a school night. They arrived to find the infamous DCI who had just brought down the Dancing Girls Killer curled up on the bottom stair, sobbing uncontrollably. The female PC — short ginger bob, compassionate beyond her years — led Cara gently to bed and somehow she sank into oblivion and then she woke up and thought that it was day two.

Now it was day 732. Cara finished her breakfast and put the cereal bowl and coffee cup straight into the dishwasher. Then she wet a cloth and wiped down the splash of coffee, the specs of granola, the ring the milk bottle had made on the counter. By nature, Cara was more one for doing the dishes only once she had run out of anything to eat from. More than once in her life, she had nipped to M&S for a six pack of whatever pants were on sale when she realised she didn't have any clean and no time to run the washing machine. But Stellan liked things just so.

'You are so from the land of IKEA,' Cara had grinned, shaking her head, when she caught him coming home with an organiser for the cutlery drawer a week or two after they got back from their honeymoon. Cara had always just tossed the lot in a heap, trusting herself to find the required utensil as necessary.

Stellan had just chuckled in that good natured way he had. 'Well now you can find one more quickly,' he said.

'Which will be a blessing in a teaspoon related emergency,' she said, standing on tiptoe to kiss the nape of his neck as he created order in her chaos. 'I'm glad you're around,' she whispered.

Now he hadn't been around for 732 days. Cara kept the house obsessively neat, as though at any moment she would hear him mutter *Car-ra* when he happened upon her mess, hitting the R in that Swedish way that made her tummy flip. That way, he would know she hadn't given up on him.

RUARI HAD NEVER GIVEN much thought to how he looked. His face was just sort of there, in the bathroom mirror every morning. He was far from sure he had a strong opinion on it either way.

His ex-girlfriend Aoife had had a thing about her nose. She thought it was too upturned, but though Ruari tried to see what she meant, and made what he hoped were the appropriate reassuring noises, he had in fact been baffled. A face was just a face, was it not? When she was drunk once, Aoife had told him that he would be almost ridiculously good looking if only his nose were slightly bigger. A bit stung, he'd muttered that she was nose-obsessed and they'd gone into such a fit of giggles that they could hardly stagger from the taxi when it pulled up outside their flat and had ended up sprawled on the pavement laughing helplessly.

He'd thought Aoife's face was lovely, but then he'd thought that Aoife was lovely. Later, he thought Lorna's face was lovely, even though she insisted it was boring. He had never got the chance to tell her it was lovely because she was murdered the night before he finally plucked up the courage to tell her how he felt.

Ages ago, around the time of Greer's trial, Ruari had had a nightmare about Lorna. In the dream, she was everywhere he looked, and her face was anything but lovely. Eyes shining black in empty sockets, flesh rotting and curdling and dripping from her skeleton, she sat behind him on the bus, glared at him from across the pub, gave him the finger from behind a treadmill at the gym. Each time he spotted her, she was a tiny bit closer and he knew that eventually she was going to grab him and punish him for making such a bloody great meal out of finding her killer that her sister was now in prison. Just as Lorna finally reached for him, he had woken up screaming and Hannah was there.

Ruari had reached out to Hannah a few weeks after their one night stand. He tracked her down on Facebook to apologise about being such a weirdo that morning, and she'd laughed it off and pointed out that she owed him a stick of chewing gum and a coffee. After a few weeks of messaging back and forth, they met for a drink, and somehow fell into something that was nice and relaxed.

'Friends with benefits plus,' Hannah proclaimed one night over a Chinese takeaway. 'That covers it quite well. No, wait — how about Premium friends with benefits?'

'Aye, that sounds good.'

Then Ruari nicked the last spring roll and she cheerfully pronounced him downgraded to human vibrator.

A few weeks later he'd woken up screaming after his nightmare about Lorna, and for the rest of the night she held him and stroked his hair as he poured out the entire story. They hadn't got around to updating their label, but Ruari thought that Hannah's face was lovely.

He still didn't have a particularly strong opinion of his own, but he had recently learned it was ideal for private investigation. 'Aye, you'll do fine, son,' the wee guy who'd handed him his license told him. 'Nobody would remember you five minutes after meeting you.'

'Thanks very much.'

The wee guy was far from Hollywood's idea of a private detective, slight and balding with light grey eyes that peered from behind steel rimmed glasses. He looked more like a tax inspector or the ticket man on the train, but, as he explained, that was the point.

'Ach I'm sure you've got a sparkling personality, son, but 90% of what we do is surveillance. Just being there to see what's going on, what somebody is up to, and reporting back. Never mind all your high tech equipment they have these days, nothing beats your own eyes and ears -- and the only way to get to watch and listen is if nobody notices you. Human wallpaper, that's the ticket. That's the difference between us and the police. They're all about being seen to do the job. They patrol the streets in their high vis get-ups and whip out sirens to let the world know they're on their way. We stay in the shadows.'

Ruari yawned now, wondering how much longer he should hang about. He'd been leaning against a pub door-way, pretending to smoke, for several hours. There hadn't been a sign of movement from the flat he was watching.

The day had been warm, with even a hint of summer in the air. Earlier, Ruari had done paperwork in the garden for a couple of hours in the wee garden at the back close and his nose itched with the sting of sunburn. Now though, the late afternoon air had a distinct nip in it. He stamped his feet to warm up as he fiddled with his lighter and scanned the street again. Nothing.

Though he was confident the occupant of the flat wasn't going anywhere in a hurry, he decided to give it another hour. He yawned again, thinking that at least Hannah would be home to get dinner started by the time he got in. She was a brilliant cook, forever experimenting with spices and herbs and all manner of kitchen utensils Ruari couldn't make head nor tail of. His fish fingers had long since been banished from her domain. He yawned and stamped his feet, feeling as though his joints were creaking like old door hinges. Maybe he'd give it a bit longer than an hour, he thought.

CARA HADN'T BEEN in court to hear the verdict on the case she had been investigating for months. She had been planning to be there, but she had been held up by the meeting she dreaded every week, the check in with her boss, Detective Superintendent Liam Kavanagh.

Liam was a few years older than her. She had noticed a suspicious immobility about his eyes and forehead the last time they met, which ironically made him look older than the mid-forties or so he must be. Cara and Liam had come up through the ranks together for the first decade or so of their careers, until sometime in their early thirties when it was as though his caught a wind while hers sprang a slow leak.

Cara had been one of the youngest women ever to be appointed Detective Chief Inspector in Police Scotland, and she still outranked the vast majority of women on the force. She wouldn't want the largely office-based role of Superintendent, she'd told herself many a time. Being relegated to a desk job would bore her senseless in days. But she'd still like the chance to turn it down, that wee voice in her head whispered. Her weekly forelock-tugging session in front of a guy she'd put in the recovery position after he downed a pint of whisky on a dare once upon a time, didn't help.

It was late, she realised now as she flew up the front steps of the High Court. Most trials had finished for the day. There was just one bored security guard left. He gave Cara's bag a desultory glance and waved her through the metal detector. Cara's footsteps echoed up the quiet corridor as she dashed towards the courtroom.

It wasn't her job to pay attention to the trials of cases she investigated, yet still she knew this building like the back of her hand. Other than giving evidence when asked, she was supposed to wash her hands of a given investigation as soon as she handed her recommendation up to the procurator fiscal, but Cara rarely could. She didn't consider her job complete until a guilty verdict was handed down.

She caught sight of the victim's family huddled outside the courtroom, and saw it before they even turned towards her. Misery and defeat emanated from their stooped shoulders and bent heads, and Cara's heart fell. The victim's mother was dry-eyed and stoic, flanked on either side by tall sons.

Whoops and backslaps from the defendant's family echoed in Cara's ears as she quickened her pace. *What happened?* she wondered desperately. She hadn't thought the verdict would be so much as in question. He had shown pictures, gruesome and heartbreaking, on his phone around the pub. 'That'll fuckin' teach her,' he crowed, and the wee barmaid had taken out her own phone and subtly filmed his horrific boasts.

'You said he'd go to jail,' the mother moaned as Cara approached. 'You said he'd go away for a long time.'

'Aye, I — I don't know what — I'm so, so sorry, let me speak to the crown advocate, see what —'

'Is it not your job to put him in the jail?' one of the brothers demanded. His height made him look like a man, but close up Cara could see a frightened wee boy, his voice hoarse with unshed tears. 'What is your fuckin' job if not to put scum like that behind bars?'

'My job is to try my best to put scum like that behind bars,' Cara said evenly. 'But the verdict is out my hands. Let me try to find out what happened.'

'Well you're fuckin' shite at your job,' the brother shouted. His face crumpled and he howled, turned and kicked a gleaming oak bench. 'You should fuckin' be behind bars, you useless bitch.'

'I am so sorry,' Cara said again, wanting to reach out and hug him.

'Don't mind him,' the victim's mother — Cara realised with a flush of mortification that she couldn't remember her name — whispered. 'He's just a wee bit upset.'

'He has every right to be upset,' said Cara. 'You all do. Sometimes —' she began, then sighed, knowing fine there were no words that could comfort. She felt like crying herself. This verdict was supposed to be a win. She heard the defendant laugh as he and his crew made their way out into the late afternoon sunshine, and she wanted to run over and slam his head into the marble wall. 'Sometimes the system gets it wrong. I don't know what happened.'

'Thought you were supposed to be the hotshot?' the other brother, older with a military buzz cut and shattered eyes, said quietly. He was still holding on to his mother's arm. It struck Cara that the mother was barely a year or two older than her. 'They told us that with you in charge our Katie would get justice. But she's not, has she?'

'I —' Cara began.

'We know you're sorry. We heard you the first hundred and five times.'

'COME ON GUYS, pick up the pace — break in thirty seconds if you earn it!'

Jade was rewarded with a collective groan from the array of red, sweating bodies clad in bright and sparkling leotards and leggings. She had come up with the idea of a retro *Keep Fit* class when she was cleaning out her old room at her granny's before selling the flat. In a box in the cupboard of her old bedroom, she stumbled across the luminous pink weights, matching sweatband and glittery ribbon stick that were her idea of fitness when she was a wee girl.

She pitched the idea to the manager of one of her regular gyms, told folk to come in their most shocking eighties get-ups and devised routines to classic Madonna and Kylie that cleverly hid burpees and lunges and squats in a vintage boogie. 'A bit like putting a dog's medicine in cheese,' she imagined telling Gran with a satisfied grin. There was a waiting list every week. She was currently on a mission to get the gym manager to agree to let her bring a disco ball, but so far he kept muttering about not taking things too far.

'Okay guys one minute — grab some water.'

She crouched on the stage and picked up her phone, scrolled through the playlist she spent way more time glee-fully building than she should. She had been planning to go on to *I Want to Dance with Somebody,* but could sense the group flagging. A wee bit of Abba would soon see to that, she thought.

A thud resounded round the studio as somebody dropped their water bottle. Jade froze, her heart thumping, pins and needles stinging her fingers. *Take a Chance on Me*, she thought, but she had forgotten what those words meant.

'Have I got time to nip to the toilet?' one of the regulars was suddenly in front of her, too close, grinning manically in her face. 'I took that much water I'm pure burstin'.'

'No — no, I'm sorry — I've got to go.' *Shit.* She was due at the police station. How could she have forgotten? What time was it? She was late, she was sure of it. *Andy*. Hot tears leapt into her eyes as she remembered he had chucked her.

'I'm sorry — I'm so sorry —'

'Oh, Jade, pet, listen — remember how you get these funny wee —'

Jade backed away then turned and broke into a run, shoving open the heavy door.

'Oh for Christ's sake is that her aff again?' someone shouted and Jade wanted to explain that she needed to get to the police station but she didn't have time.

The lights in the corridor were too bright, a group of people waiting for a *Legs, Bums and Tums* class to start in the next studio were all in her way as she fumbled with clumsy fingers, wondering why she didn't have her locker key on her. It didn't matter. She didn't need her jacket. She could come back and get it later, once she had spoken to the police. And Andy, she thought, a rush of pure pain slamming her, churning in her guts and suddenly she was sobbing.

'Jade, c'mere and sit down,' a gentle voice she vaguely recognised floated above her head. Her heart was racing, she didn't know why. Her tummy clenched and twisted as she saw Andy in her mind's eye, smiling at her in that soft way he never would again. He didn't want her any more, she thought, and hot tears sprang into her eyes.

'Take a wee sip of water,' the voice spoke again, and Jade vaguely realised she was sitting on one of the hard benches.

'You don't understand, I need to get to the police station —' Her voice wavered as another sob crashed over her. 'I'm so sorry, I can't believe I'm — I split up with my boyfriend yesterday and I'm just a bit —' Pins and needles rampaged through her chest, creating an unbearable pressure. This was what a broken heart felt like, she thought.

'I know. It's okay. You've got time to get to the police. They'll wait.'

Jade's blurred vision cleared and she realised she knew the man who was crouched in front of her holding out a water bottle. Bobby. Gentle giant Bobby. He'd been one of the regulars for donkey's years.

He definitely put the hours in, dutifully showing up at 6am on the dot every morning to train for an hour and a half before work, greeting staff with a *morning, part-timers* if they shuffled in at 6:03. The last time Jade had seen him, though, she had noticed a slight tremor in his hand when he picked up his water that suggested his gains weren't entirely down to dedication. She'd made a mental note to have a wee chat with him, which she hadn't got around to doing yet.

'I'm late,' she muttered. 'I'm sure I'm late.'

'Aye I know, just another wee sip of water.'

But the clouds were starting to clear and suddenly Jade wasn't so sure that she was late after all. In fact, wasn't there something else she was supposed to be doing? *Andy.* A fresh wave of pain hit her and her face crumpled again.

'Shit, I'm so sorry, I hate being this pathetic,' she

babbled, forcing a smile as a sob shuddered through her. 'I'm not normally like this, I've always been a total love 'em and leave 'em type but I just — I wasn't expecting — I thought things were fine between us. I feel like I've been hit by a bus. Bloody men, eh?'

'That's how you know you were really in love,' Bobby said with a smile. He sat on the bench next to Jade, rubbed her back with his huge hand. 'Some clever auld bastard said something like *he who is wise in love has never been in love.* See anyone that can keep their dignity, accept it's over right away, move on without a glance back? They're either a robot or a psychopath.'

Jade laughed through her tears. 'Well I'm definitely no' keeping a shred of dignity.'

'Then congratulations, you're a member of the human race.'

Andy's girlfriend had a baby.

The thought popped into her head out of nowhere, and for a minute it stumped her, because wasn't she Andy's girlfriend and she definitely didn't have a baby.

No, she wasn't Andy's girlfriend. She hadn't been Andy's girlfriend for two years.

That realisation slid through her like cold slime.

It had happened again.

'Bobby —' she began, mortified because this kind man was comforting her when the truth was she was only upset because her brain was fucked. 'I — the thing is —'

'That you back with us?' Bobby asked gently. He squeezed her shoulder. 'Do you know Jade, I'm in awe of you. If I got slammed with the same heartbreak over and over for years, I'd never get out my bed, honest to god, I wouldn't. But you get up every day and carry on, it's pure incredible.'

So he knew. Jade sighed. She always felt slightly shaky and lightheaded after an episode, as though she had been woken suddenly from a deep sleep. The idea of never getting out of bed seemed suddenly compelling, but she got up, handed Bobby his water bottle back.

'I'd better go and see if any of my class is left,' she said, hearing the tremor in her voice. She'd feel better when she was blaring a bit of Abba, she thought. She always did. 'Thanks Bobby. See you in the gym tomorrow?'

'Bright and early,' he grinned, saluting her. 'Be good, eh?'

3

K irsten Cameron was eighteen years old and she was raging. She'd been a legal adult for a grand total of six and a bit hours, and so far, it was shite.

She had insisted on having her party the night before her birthday, even though it was a Thursday night and some of her class still had exams. She'd had a vision of everyone doing a toast at midnight when she turned eighteen and she would have her first official drink - even though she'd be well steaming by then -- and everyone would go mad and it would be brilliant. Those who had an exam the next day would just have to decide what their priorities were, and don't think Kirsten wouldn't remember.

She had been in agonies all week, deciding which of her anthems she would instruct the DJ to play on the dot of midnight. It had to be something pure banging, because she fully intended to dance to it with Tariq in front of everyone. They would have been wynching all night already, she resolved, and it would be like their coming out.

This wasn't just her being arrogant. She'd never even imagined he would agree to come to her party, but when he texted back 'yeah' to the invitation three weeks ago — one of the very first to RSVP, by the way — she had known for sure she hadn't been imagining he was into her. She nearly started jumping up and down on the bus. All those wee looks he gave her in assembly, that time he'd wolf whistled her when she had to kick the ball in front of everyone in PE. Those three joke texts he had forwarded to her — admittedly, to a whole group, but he chose to include her — they *had* all meant what she hoped.

He was coming to her party because he liked her. It was so obvious. They were going to get together and have the most amazing summer, and maybe even get a flat in September when she started work at her auntie's beauty salon. Kirsten had zero intention of spending her entire life waxing strangers' bits, but a definite job to go to got her da off her back and it wasn't a bad wee wage. She could definitely afford half a flat with Tariq, whose parents would sub him because he was carrying on to university to do something with computers.

The only minor flaw in her plan, it turned out, was Eilidh. Eilidh was supposed to be Kirsten's friend and not a two-timing bitch, except apparently this was not the case. Eilidh had spent the whole night basically attached to Tariq, latching onto him before Kirsten had even got a chance to talk to him. The last thing Kirsten heard someone say before she stormed out was that apparently Tariq and Eilidh were getting a flat together. Kirsten hated them both and hoped their flat burned down.

Now she'd been storming along quiet roads for hours and wasn't even sure where she was. It was nearly dawn when she reached Victoria Park and realised that she'd gone miles in the wrong direction. Her feet were pure killing her and she was freezing and hungry and knackered. How could they do that to her, at her own party?

Tariq had given her this sheepish wee smile when they arrived, and that was the worst bit. He was embarrassed. He knew she was going to be upset. They'd probably discussed how to break it to her, then decided they didn't care enough to bother. Every time Kirsten pictured his face she wanted to curl up in a wee ball and cry.

Well that was it. None of them would even see her again. There was some prizegiving shite on at school next week, but Kirsten wouldn't even go and they would all just have to wonder where she was.

Kirsten wasn't sure when she became aware that somebody was behind her.

She was caught up in a fantasy of Tariq running after her, saying that Eilidh had forced him into being with her somehow, but he'd escaped and come after Kirsten because he was mad about her. When she first noticed the footsteps, for a mad moment she thought that it was him and her tummy twisted and leapt into her throat.

Then she realised that the footsteps were way too heavy to be Tariq's. Tariq kind of loped, this uneven slouchy stroll a bit like a panther or something, and was sexy as. This person walked softly, but their footsteps were even. Boring.

Kirsten started to feel irritated at this person invading her misery. You would have thought that the one upside of raging through Victoria Park in the wee hours with toes so cold she felt as though she could snap them right off would be the luxury of solitude. But no, now the bloody great fud was breathing practically right in her ear too. *Get tae fuck, roaster* she thought as the footsteps continued to approach. *Do I look sociable to you at the minute?*

She whirled around, ready to give whoever it was laldy

for getting in her face when she wasn't in the mood, when a dog started barking and she nearly jumped out of her skin. The person following her turned out to be a youngish guy with a baseball cap pulled low over his face. He was frowning at his phone, earphones in, totally ignoring the mental dog who was practically doing cartwheels to get his attention.

He hadn't even noticed Kirsten.

Obviously.

Nobody ever noticed Kirsten. Her own party was probably still raging on without her, with no one even realising that she was gone. Kirsten blinked back hot tears and wished her mum would come and get her.

There was a woman a few metres behind them, one of those mental keen folk who jog at the crack of dawn. She had long red hair tied back in a messy ponytail and was nearly hidden beneath a huge grey hoodie that just about reached her knees. She was looking at Kirsten with concern in her eyes. Brilliant. All Kirsten needed was pity from some nutcase who voluntarily got out of bed to come over all sweaty and out of puff at this absurd hour.

The dog walker finally glanced up, startled when he caught sight of Kirsten standing in the path in front of him. He started to smile, a polite, stranger smile, until his eyes moved past her and he screamed instead.

'Don't look - don't look —' he yelled, yanking Kirsten by the arm as his bloody dog yapped like a halfwit.

But Kirsten looked and she would never forget what she saw for the rest of her life.

'YOU'D BETTER NOT EVEN BE LOOKING at that bloody rowing machine,' Maggie warned.

'Ach you love it really,' Jade grinned as she programmed in three 500 metre intervals.

Maggie was one of Jade's favourite clients. Jade had been delighted when Maggie announced at their introductory session that she didn't give a monkey's what she weighed or what she looked like in a bikini (or anything else for that matter) she just wanted to be able to dance all night.

She was making up for lost time, she explained. Her husband had left her the year before, and at first Maggie had been heartbroken and lost, gutted by the taint Joe's embarrassing behaviour had put on three decades of memories. A few weeks later, her pals dragged her along to a psychic night at their local and the psychic announced she saw a lot of fun in Maggie's future. It hit Maggie then that she couldn't remember the last time she had had fun without Joe's face tripping him.

In the taxi home that night she resolved that if she was going to head into her dotage on her ownsome, she was going to do it in style. Since then she'd revelled in reading into the wee hours with no one to complain about the bedside light, ordered takeaway for breakfast and munched cereal for dinner if she felt like it, and taught students younger than her own kids a thing or two about how to dance the night away in the same Sauchiehall Street dives she had been the queen of in the seventies.

Just before her birthday a couple of months ago — it was a big one, she admitted, though she declined to confirm which one — she confided in her eldest daughter that she wished Joe had done his runner ten years earlier when she still had the energy for single life. The daughter, being a no-problems-only-challenges type, decided that age was no match for stamina, and rounded up her siblings to club together for six months of personal training with Jade for their mum's birthday.

'Okay, full on sprint for the last hundred metres,' Jade announced now as Maggie huffed and puffed on the rowing machine.

'Bugger off,' grinned Maggie, but she obeyed.

'You've got it in you. Just a few more seconds now, nae bother —'

'I'll nae bother you,' muttered Maggie, and Jade reminded her that if she could talk she wasn't working hard enough. Maggie shot her an evil look and Jade blew her a kiss and Maggie finished her five hundred metres in just under three minutes.

'Whatever happened with the guy you were telling me about, that you met on the bus the other week?' asked Jade as Maggie gulped down some water and wiped her sweat-sodden fringe from her forehead.

'Oh God wait till you hear it, you'll scream.'

Maggie launched in to the story of how she and the man from the bus had gone for one okay-ish drink and she was quite looking forward to seeing him again when out of the blue he started texting her a series of unintentionally hilarious erotic fantasies.

'I mean, it would have been one thing if we'd got a bit of sexy banter going, but at the pub it was aw' polite chit chat, dead boring, nothing in that direction at all. So here was me thinking we didn't fancy each other, but maybe we could be pals and see from there, when all of a sudden he starts firing fifty shades of shite at me.'

As Maggie paused for a sip of water, Jade noticed a wee crowd congregated around the front desk. She frowned as she Maggie picked up her story. There had been talk of staff lay-offs over the past few months. It wouldn't directly affect

Jade as she was self employed with her own clients, but a bad atmosphere was never ideal for anyone.

Jade still felt a bit grouchy and out of sorts after the day before's battery of episodes. She kept thinking it was getting better, that she was getting it under control, then she'd hit a nasty patch and feel back to square one. Jade had never been a great fan of dogs. It wasn't as though she wished them harm or anything, she just found them a bit smelly and annoying and terrible at taking the hint when a person really didn't want a great slobbery nose in their face, thank you very much. For reasons of not wishing folk to think her a monster, she generally kept that fact to herself, but it pleased her, in a vaguely defying society kind of way, to think of the terror as a big annoying dog.

For two years it had followed her incessantly, intent on shoving its slobbery nose in her face no matter how many times she told it to bugger off. Sometimes, when she had really shouted at it, it kept its distance for a while, though even then it hovered just in the corner of her eye so as to remind her that it was never truly gone. Occasionally, she thought she had it under control. It was there, but it was trotting obediently to heel, staying at a safe, steady distance. But that never lasted. Every time she convinced herself she had won, that she had broken the mutt in, it would leap at her out of nowhere and knock her flat, slam her brain right back to when it happened, as though as punishment for being so stupid as to imagine herself leader of their pack of two.

'The last one was all about us getting down to it on a beach,' Maggie's voice pierced Jade's thoughts and she forced herself back to the present. 'Just as I was thinking, Christ that's one way to be finding sand in your unmentionables forevermore, I read the immortal line — are you ready for this?'

Jade grinned and nodded. Maggie's stories were always good for a bit of distraction.

'*I'll be as hard as the cliffs and you'll be as wet as the ocean.* I mean, bless his wee bum but for goodness' sake.'

Jade snorted with laughter. 'Oh no, you're joking. Please let that not be true. I don't want to live in a world where a man thinks that's acceptable patter.'

'Me neither, pet. Me neither.'

'I mean — the ocean?'

'I know. I know.' Maggie held up her hands in surrender. 'I don't know what to tell you. It's a terrible world we live in.'

'Well now you've traumatised me for life, that's you done for today. 'Mon over for a wee stretch.'

A few minutes later, Jade was still chuckling as she waved Maggie off and wandered over to the desk to write up her notes for Maggie's next session. The wee crowd had dispersed, but two of the gym instructors, Maddie and Kåre, were still huddled together deep in conversation.

'Have you heard?' demanded Maddie as Jade approached. She was Aussie and after years in Glasgow still looked as though she'd just stepped off Bondi Beach thanks to an admirable dedication to sun beds and bleach. Kåre, a tall Norwegian weightlifter who Jade suspected was the primary reason for the gym's healthy female population, rubbed Maddie's shoulder, his expression grim.

'Heard what?' asked Jade with a yawn, refilling her water bottle. Her first client on a Friday was a company director who could only fit her in at 5:45am, and there wasn't enough coffee in the world to make that palatable.

'You know Bobby?'

'Yeah, of course.' Jade flushed, remembering how he had held her hand the day before.

'They found him in Victoria Park this morning.' Maddie continued, her voice wavering.

'What do you mean, found him?'

'He's dead.' Maddie burst into tears, evidently not for the first time that day.

Jade stared at her, stunned fury churning in her gust. *Fucking steroids*, she thought bitterly, picturing Bobby's heart giving out while on his evening run. Kåre gathered Maddie into his arms, but Jade backed away, trembling with rage at the fucking waste, the fucking stupidity of trying to cheat body chemistry. *Aye, you're ripped enough now*, she thought furiously. *You stupid bawbag. Ripped and dead.*

'The police want to talk to anybody that knew him,' Kåre was saying in his soft Norwegian accent. 'I think your name was on the list Jade, so probably they will call you.'

Caught up in her fury, Jade barely heard him. 'The police?' she repeated in surprise. 'What are you talking about? What for?'

'Because he was murdered.'

CARA WAS LOATHE to resort to the grainy sludge that passed for coffee from the office machine, but she'd left it too late to send a constable to pick her up something drinkable before the meeting. At this point, she decided, caffeine that made her wonder if there was a dead squirrel in the pot was better than no caffeine at all.

The team were already gathered and waiting expectantly when she slipped in to the back of the room, flashing an apologetic smile at DI Samira Shah who stood at the front of the room. That morning in Victoria Park, Cara had assigned Samira to take the lead on this investigation.

A couple of years previously, Samira had inadvertently allowed Alec McAvoy to listen in to the investigative team's every conversation after absentmindedly leaving Crowded Room, the dating app McAvoy used to stalk potential victims on her phone. Ever since, she had been working seemingly inhuman hours, volunteering manpower to teams in their department that were short staffed, in addition to the cases she was officially working. Most recently, she had embarked on her Masters in Criminal Psychology around her shifts. Where she found the hours, never mind the energy, Cara had no idea.

For the last several months, Cara had been regularly recommending her for promotion. Liam's argument that he didn't have the budget to raise Samira's pay grade wore thin when he approved the promotions of two male DIs in other departments, so recently he had switched to citing the Crowded Room app incident as proof Samira wasn't ready for the next rank.

It wasn't just good old fashioned sexism, Cara thought in frustration. It was bloody-mindedness. Alec McAvoy had been one of Liam's cronies. He hated that Cara had been right about him. She hadn't given up on Samira's promotion, she just had to think of a a way of presenting it to Liam that he couldn't wriggle his way out of.

'So what are we looking at?' she asked now, sipping the godawful coffee with a grimace as she leaned against the back wall.

'Bobby O'Brien,' began Samira. 'Thirty-two, freelance joiner, worked mostly on his own, occasionally contracted by firms. He grew up around Lambhill and moved to Scotstoun about ten years ago. Single. There was an engagement to a childhood sweetheart, but they went their separate ways three years ago. Seems to have been all very amicable, he is godfather to her baby.

'He was found this morning in Victoria Park by a dog walker and a teenage girl.' Samira switched the overhead projector on, nodded at the young constable by the door to dim the lights. 'Guys, I know some of you were at the scene, but for anyone who wasn't, these photos are — not pleasant. If anyone needs to leave the room for a moment, please do. It will be a lot less disruptive than you staying and puking or passing out.'

A muted chuckle rumbled round the room. Cara caught one of the guys from the data media unit glancing over at DC Lauren McNabb, who was listening attentively, her hair in its usual long blonde plait. He wouldn't leave the room unless she did, Cara thought, only just suppressing an eye roll.

Though she was just a couple of years on the force, both of Lauren's parents were coppers, it was in her blood. Her dad Iain was a case manager who worked with Cara's team regularly, and her mum was a DI specialising in domestic violence. Lauren had already proven herself unflappable, and if the wee computery guy expected her to break first, he could clean up his own puke.

'As you can see here, there are certain elements consistent with an execution style killing, which could suggest organised crime.'

'What — how did — what happened to his face?' asked the data media unit guy, looking green. Cara saw DC Kevin MacGregor sidle a little closer to him, clearly preparing to catch him if he fainted.

'It was removed,' said Samira bluntly, staring at the image projected on the screen. 'Several incisions were made around the neck and the skin covering his head and face was pulled off like a sock, more or less. It has not yet been found.'

There was a collective cringe in the room, and the data media guy made a dash for the door, crashing into the door-frame in his haste.

'Could someone go after him and make sure he doesn't hit his head on anything if he passes out?' said Cara mildly. Lauren was closest to the door. She rolled her eyes, then scuttled out. Cara just caught her exasperated 'fuck's sake, man,' before the door swung shut.

'We've started looking into potential links to organised crime,' Samira continued as though nothing has happened, 'but Bobby O'Brien's financial records are unremarkable. No' much the way of savings but no real debt to speak of. Mortgage, average credit cards he paid a decent chuck off of every month. No dodgy loans or anything to suggest the kind of financial trouble that might lead him down that path, and no other connections we have found so far. He has a brother who's been in the Bar-L a couple of times, but —'

'Could he have been involved in anything organised?' Kevin asked.

'Well his first stretch was for driving his car through a Tescos window, grabbing all he could carry in his arms and making a run for it. Police followed a trail of dropped bags of Hula Hoops until they caught up with him round the corner about ten minutes later. Second time, he fell asleep in the middle of robbing a house and only woke up when he was handcuffed.'

'Doesnae scream mafia,' Kevin pronounced around a mouthful of biscuit.

'Aye, thanks for your insight there Kevin. Still though, slit throat, these, umm, particular injuries to the face — let's keep the possible mob theory in mind for now. Alison Crawford is hoping to join us as soon as she can, but in the meantime I can pass on that she has confirmed the fatal injury is this cut to the neck here, made with an extremely sharp knife, which severed the cartroid arteries. Blood loss would loss would have been severe and catastrophic. Alison judges that Bobby O'Brien will have lost consciousness within seconds. Another thing that suggests this killer knew what they were doing. Small mercies.'

Cara agreed. Even she had to concentrate to keep her breathing steady as she forced herself to look at the close up of what was once the man's face. It had to be personal, she thought. Surely you had to know someone to do that to them.

'The other thing we need to keep in mind is that close ups I've shown so far do not convey the victim's size,' added Samira. 'To be blunt, Bobby O'Brien was massive. He was a big guy to start with, and he obviously put in serious hours at the gym. He was pure muscle, looked like he could snap somebody's neck with one hand.' Samira paused, looked around the room, her eyes grave. 'It is difficult to imagine just who could have overpowered him and how, not to mention why he didn't put up a fight and escape. There are no defensive injuries on the body. I suspect that these aspects will prove key to finding his killer.

'It's early days and let's keep our minds open, but for my money, it does not seem likely a killer would select Bobby O'Brien as a victim without a very powerful and specific reason.' Samira clicked off the projector and there was a exhalation of relief.

'One thing that might be nothing but I'm just putting it out there,' she continued. 'He knew Jade McFadyen.

'If you remember, Jade McFadyen was attacked and

managed to escape on the same night that Alec McAvoy was caught. At the time, we were worried it was a sign that he had another puppet out there we'd missed.'

Cara noticed Kevin shifting uncomfortably, his eyes on the ground. Kevin McGregor had veered dangerously close to inadvertently becoming one of Alec McAvoy's puppets. 'Jade has little to no memories of the attack and has not been able to provide us with a description. We haven't identified her attacker, but it's been two years now and there have been no similar attacks.'

'How do they know each other?' asked Lauren, slipping back into the room.

'He goes to the gym where she is a personal trainer. It seems he was quite the regular and pally with a few of the staff, including Jade. One of the managers put together an initial list of folk to talk to for us, and she was on it. I've confirmed it's the same Jade McFadyen.'

'Could well be a coincidence especially given how much time has passed,' mused Cara. 'However at this stage everything's worth checking into. Samira, why don't you have a chat with her yourself? Maybe take Lauren.'

Samira nodded. 'Yeah that's what I was thinking too. There is one more thing —' she added. A few people had started to shift, apparently sensing the meeting was about to wind up. Samira paused, waiting until the room fell quiet and still again. Cara had long since given up bothering to be annoyed by her flare for the dramatic.

Samira switched the projector back on and clicked to the final image of the set. It was a drone shot looking down on the body from a few metres above. It was the first time they had seen the entire body. A palpable sense of horror permeated the room as everyone took in the image in silence.

Bobby O'Brien's arms formed an elegant arc just in front

of his waist, as though he were holding an invisible beach ball. His legs were tightly together, heels touching, his toes pointing outwards in a horizontal line.

Cara had lasted a week at the ballet lessons her mum sent her to when she was about six, before getting in trouble for making farting noises in time to the music as the class pliéed, and being asked to leave. A couple of years ago, however, she had memorised every one of the ballet foundation positions when the Dancing Girls Killer was posing his victims in the positions in sequence. The last victim to be posed in this way had been Kelly Gallagher, who was posed in the fifth, and final, position.

Bobby O'Brien was posed in first position.

'SEVENTEEN VISITS,' Greer announced as Ruari handed over a paper cup of tea and took a seat at the wee table opposite her. The warden glanced over as a toddler started screaming at the table next to them. Ruari shifted uncomfortably. The seats in the prison visitors' hall were those weird shiny plastic kind that always made him feel as though he would slide right off.

'What?'

'Seventeen visits I've been putting up with your shite patter.'

'Sorry to have troubled you with the pleasure of my company.'

Greer gave him the finger in the guise of scratching her nose, took a sip of her tea and grimaced. 'Too milky.'

'Good thing there's just the one visit left then.'

Greer had been sentenced to eighteen months for shoving Alec McAvoy out the first floor window of a semi demolished building. Her solicitor had warned that it could

have been a lot worse. From that point of view, it was conve-
nient that McAvoy stubbornly clung to life in the Intensive
Care Unit of Queen Elizabeth University Hospital.

'Do you know it's called defenestration?' Greer asked
suddenly.

'What is?'

'The act of shoving somebody out a window.'

As Ruari thought this over, a pale wee guy with a
gigantic sparkly earring, wearing a green tracksuit, fell to his
knees at few tables along from them. A couple of wardens
darted forward, but he produced a ring box and started to
sing some cheesy pop hit about it being a beautiful day, in a
curiously thin and high voice.

'Christ no,' shrieked the woman he had come to visit.
She wore a strikingly ugly hand-knitted orange jumper, and
a stunning tattoo of a serpent crept up her neck. 'Whiny wee
schmout like you? Get right tae fuck and don't come back.'
She cackled wildly, swinging on the back two legs of her
chair in the manner Ruari remembered primary school
teachers issuing stark warnings against.

'You've missed out on the best chance you ever had,' the
wee guy whined and a couple of wardens firmly led him
towards the door. 'I would've loved you to the ends of the
earth and back again.' One of the wardens gave him a
sympathetic pat on the shoulder as he led him from the hall
with the woman's laughter presumably ringing in his ears.

'See with his earring and the green tracksuit?' said
Ruari, taking another sip of his tea before remembering it
was disgusting. The wee guy thumped the window from
outside and howled. 'From the side he looks like a
Christmas tree.'

'Who'd marry a man that dresses up as a Christmas tree
in May?'

'Not her apparently,' said Ruari. The woman in the orange jumper was still chortling away, sitting alone at her table. Ruari finished his overly milky tea and wished he'd grabbed a couple of biscuits. Then he thought he might get a McDonalds on the way home, and a hot dart of guilt shot through him. Greer wouldn't be able to get a cheeky McDonalds whenever she felt like it for another six weeks. 'I didn't know there was an actual name for shoving someone out a window,' he added.

'The dictionary says defenestration 'connotes the forcible or peremptory removal of an adversary,'' Greer shrugged. 'If that doesn't cover it I don't know what does.'

'What does peremptory mean?'

'It means imperious, high-handed or arrogant.' She shrugged, wiggled her eyebrows. 'That's me.'

'Naw, you weren't being arrogant,' Ruari said. 'You did it for Lorna.'

Greer fell silent a moment, then nodded towards a pale woman a few tables away. 'That woman over there, she killed a teenage boy with her car. She was stone cold sober, driving home from work late at night. She took her eyes off the road for a split second to glance at a text from her husband, and this wee boy stepped out in front of her and now he's dead.

'They give her pills to help her sleep, but even so, she wakes up screaming most nights. I was sitting next to her at lunch once, and she told me that what wakes her up is all the things he could have been.

'All that potential and possibilities for a life that she destroyed in an instant's absentmindedness. She said that she'll be in a deep sleep, and a vision will chisel its way into her brain of him having a kickabout with his own wee boy, or graduating as a doctor, or paying off his mum and dad's mortgage. All the things that will never happen now because of her. That's what eats away at her.'

Greer stared evenly at Ruari and there was a hard glint in her eye.

'But what would Alec McAvoy be doing right now if I hadn't done what I did? Even if they had got him on those surveillance charges, he could be nearly out by now. Or, if somehow they had managed to get him put away for a good few years, you know what I've learned in here? Prison doesn't stop those that know what they're doing.

'Half the women in here are still conducting whatever scam got them banged up. They've got contingency plans, second-in-charges running things on their behalf, a whole maze of codes for visits and phone call. It's like the bloody Cold War, if Russian spies had been primarily concerned with cutting coke with washing powder to sell to schemes in the East End. You think McAvoy wouldn't have something like that on the go?'

Ruari flinched, picturing McAvoy stretched comfortably on a bunk in a cell, relaxing with a good book, while dozens of his puppets roamed the streets of Glasgow.

'The only way to stop him was to do what I did,' Greer said with a quiet firmness. 'It's not like I relished it. It's not I'm planning to defenester anybody ever again, but it doesn't keep me awake at night. Sometimes you have to fight fire with fire. I did what I did and I can live with it.'

Ruari nodded.

'You know how folk say, 'if somebody hurt one of my family I wouldn't hesitate?' Well someone did, and I didn't.'

The mum at the next table was holding the toddler above her head, tickling it while it shrieked with laughter.

'Sometimes I wish it had never happened, but that's

purely selfish. It's only because if it hadn't happened I'd be out in Shoreditch right now drinking cocktails.'

'It's two o'clock in the afternoon.'

Greer shrugged. 'Ach it's always cocktail hour somewhere. Anyway, what's this I hear about you and Hannah moving in together?'

Half an hour later, Ruari tucked into his Big Mac on the bus and remembered Greer's words. 'Sometimes you have to fight fire with fire.' Ruari wasn't sure why the thought made him uncomfortable. He had always believed in law and order, long before he had a clue what the words were. A sense that there were rules and procedures that were fundamentally just and fair and if everyone just stuck to them then everything would be okay. It was why he had wanted to join the police in the first place.

But Greer was right. Alec McAvoy and the chaos he architected existed outside the normal order of things. He had caused death and destruction, and yet they had struggled to find a crime to charge him with. If Greer hadn't condemned him to a hospital bed he would still be executing his reign of terror. Even so, the idea that the only way to fight him was with fire chilled Ruari to his bones.

JADE SLIPPED around the barriers closing off Renfrew Street and stuffed her hands in her pockets. She couldn't get warm. Friday was her crazy day, with back-to-back clients from six until six then a spin class. Normally she loved that spin class. She would cheerfully announce at the start that she had been up since five and was more knackered than any of them so if anyone had a right to lag behind it was her and she would not. Then it became a race against herself, a fight to the death with her own stamina, that normally left her equally drained and elated.

But today she didn't feel anything.

Even the heartbreaking sight of the burnt out husk of the Glasgow School of Art didn't produce a thing. She was just cold. And numb.

One Saturday morning when Jade was thirteen or fourteen, she was shopping with her gran on Duke Street when a car mounted the pavement just in front of them and smashed into a shop window. What Jade mostly remembered was the way the sound of the crash physically reverberated through her. She felt it in her bones, heard it only hours later ringing in her ears. The world went into surreal slow motion as she absorbed the almighty bang, even as Gran yanked her out of harm's way and told her *no' tae staun' there like a numpty*.

That's how she felt about the news of Bobby's death. She couldn't grasp it. The unreality of it was zinging, echoing through her, consuming her even as she struggled to hear it. All afternoon, every time she had 30 seconds free, she had caught herself scrolling through the outpouring of grief and shock piling up on his Facebook wall, trying to get it through her thick skull that it was real.

It was daft, she told herself, and even the voice in her head didn't sound like her. She hardly knew the guy. What was he to her? They'd passed the time of day a handful of times over the years, but she'd never laid eyes on him outside the gym. She'd given him a few pointers on his form here and there, and and he had talked her out of an episode once or twice. It was a terrible thing that had happened, a kind man lost to the world in such a horrible way, but it really didn't have anything to do with her.

Except that it was supposed to be her.

What a load of shite, she thought irritably, shaking her head as though to physically dislodge the thought. *Myopic shite at that*, she added. The poor man was actually dead and all she could think was that she could have been. She caught a woman giving her a funny look as she passed, and suddenly felt an absurd urge to stick her tongue out at her. She turned onto Sauchiehall Street and remembered too late that it too was all cordoned off for roadworks. She'd have to veer on down to Bath Street or cut up shadowy lanes that stank of rubbish and piss. Fabulous.

A guy she vaguely knew had been murdered two years after she was attacked. One had nothing to do with the other. Wasn't this city supposed to be the murder capital of something-or-other? As she negotiated her way through the dizzying maze of pedestrian walkways circumventing various craters in the road, she thought she remembered that was a myth. That, despite its reputation, Glasgow's violent crime rate was practically middling these days.

All the same, an attempted murder and a murder separated by two years were perfectly standard for any city. She was just stunned because it was a terrible shame. Bobby was a nice person, and now he was gone. Anybody would feel wobbly at that.

Folk react to shock in all sorts of ways, her first therapist had intoned to her. *There is no right or wrong way.* She had chucked him when he kept insisting she try to recreate a panic attack in his office so that he could talk her through it and she would see that there was nothing to be afraid of.

'You're quite safe,' he said with a patronising smile, peering at her over half moon glasses she suspected he thought made him look intellectual. 'Nobody has ever died from a panic attack before.'

'I know,' Jade hissed at him with clenched teeth. 'I'm not scared of them. I just want to make them go away.'

'Panic attacks can be truly terrifying —'

'Aye, but like I've just said —'

'And once we face our fear of them, we can begin to —'

Jade got up and walked out. She'd tried one more therapist, a woman who wore hippy dippy caftans and whose eyes filled up when Jade started to explain why she was there, then she decided she was done. She didn't want sympathetic tears, she definitely didn't want patronising mansplaining, she just wanted her bloody brain back.

Her reaction to the news of Bobby's death was to feel nothing, and that was the right reaction because there were no wrong ones, she thought, as she finally escaped the orange plastic labyrinth and headed for Sauchiehall Lane.

At the entrance of the lane she stopped short, almost physically recoiled as though a magnetic field were repelling her.

It was too dark in there, she thought frantically, even though it wasn't. Anyone could be behind that skip, slinking in those doorways. *Aye,* she told herself fiercely, *your standard drunken randoms who couldn't give a single baw hair about anybody passing by. Fuck's sake, Jade, pull yourself together.*

She felt his icy hands slither around her ankle and she broke into a sprint. She zig zagged amongst other displaced pedestrians, nearly skidding on a slimy bit of lettuce scattered in front of a restaurant skip. *I've got bloody leggings on,* she told herself ferociously, desperately, as she ran. *I wouldn't feel his hands even if they were around my ankles.* Still, she ran.

A delivery lorry loomed in front of her, blocking the whole alley. *Shit, shit.* A palpable wall of terror slammed her as she realised she was trapped. Then at the last second she spotted a sliver of daylight beyond the lorry and slipped around it, thumping against the cold metal, scraping her shoulder on the viscous wall.

'Go round the other side, ya tube.'. Did someone say that? She didn't know, couldn't see.

Hot pins and needles fizzed in her guts, every cell in her body zinged with the need to escape. She finally passed the lorry and nearly cried with relief as she spotted the end of the alleyway up ahead. If she could just get there she would be able to breathe again.

Everything was fine. She was just a bit claustrophobic. Loads of folk got claustrophobia. It was totally normal. Her friend Hannah got so freaked out when they locked the doors of the plane before takeoff, that when they went to Australia when they were eighteen she took her jumper off and ran up the aisle, forgetting that she didn't have anything on underneath. She was wrestled back to her seat in her bra by irritated cabin crew so the plane could take off.

As Jade sprinted onto Blythswood Street she collided with a hard body. It was a man, his face half hidden under a hoody. She felt his rock hard chest and knew he could snap her in two if he wanted and blackness rushed at her like a tidal wave.

'Jeez-o, you okay there?'

Jade's knees buckled violently with a moan as her chest heaved, breath hardened in her throat and her vision tunnelled to a close. As she slipped into merciful darkness she felt herself roughly heaved off the ground.

'Can somebody phone a ambulance?' The words echoed in her ears, distant and meaningless. 'I think this lassie's fainted.'

. . .

'IT'S NOT POSSIBLE.' Cara was vaguely conscious that she was hugging herself, even though the day was uncharacteristically warm. She stood by the window of her office, staring out at the sun glinting off the murky Clyde as it snaked its way through the city. A vast blue sky awned over the city, dwarfing the dingy skyscrapers and distant rolling hills dotted with wind turbines.

Samira closed the door behind her. 'Duncan McGregor is dead,' Cara said urgently, as though daring Samira to disagree. 'It was him that put those women in ballet positions after he killed them'

Duncan McGregor was Alec McAvoy's brother, abandoned and taken into care as a young child. At some point, the two men had reconnected and Alec manipulated Duncan into carrying out a series of murders for him, first in London and then Glasgow. Duncan then took forensic psychologist Amy Kerr, who was on Alec's trail, hostage and he was killed on the island where he held her. 'The only person outside of our immediate team who knew the details of the ballet positions is Alec McAvoy himself,' Cara added.

'I spoke to the consultant overseeing McAvoy's care last week,' said Samira. 'Same story it's been for two years. There's still brain activity, he's in what they call a minimally conscious state. Technically he could open his eyes at any moment, but as yet, he has showed no signs of doing so. Lazy fuck.'

'Imagine if he was faking it,' Cara murmured, turning to look out the window again. 'All this time, just dozing and daydreaming away while nurses and doctors dance around him. He's got the stamina. He lived a double life for god knows how many years, hero barrister by day and serial killer puppeteer by night. Lying still and playing dumb would be a doddle to him.'

Samira shook her head. 'Nah,' she said. 'That's exactly it. Alec's a man of action. He craves power and excitement and control and adventure. Lying there helpless day after day? If he is conscious of it, it is driving him out of his tiny mind.'

Her smile was tinged with satisfaction. 'It's worse than prison for him, I think. In prison, he'd be king of the castle by now, not lying around getting his arse wiped. They put on radio and telly for certain patients in the ICU, one of the nurses told me, in the hopes it might stimulate the brain between visits and therapy sessions. She said they all take turns deciding what he would hate the most then leave it on for hours. They're making him binge last year's *Love Island* at the moment.'

'That's novel,' Cara said, a half-smile playing on her lips. She flopped onto her chair and put her head in her hands. 'So maybe we're right about Bobby O'Brien's murder being personal then. Maybe — maybe the positioning is a coincidence. Maybe he's just lying there and we're seeing things that aren't there.'

Samira nodded slowly. She didn't look convinced.

'What does Kevin say?'

Kevin oversaw a database, referred to as Project Club, that was tasked with gathering evidence from every person who had been a member of the Crowded Room app. The vast majority had innocently thought they were signing up for a genuine dating app, but there was a tiny set of VIP members who signed up in the hopes of getting to act out murder scenarios with willing — and sometimes unwilling — victims. Alec McAvoy used the club to hunt for potential killers to use as puppets, and though none had been active since McAvoy was caught, there was always the fear that one or two were simply dormant.

'He confirmed that not one person he has interviewed in

two years knew a thing about ballet positions. The vast majority didn't know a thing about any of it. Duncan was the only one who placed his victims that way. Did you know their mother went to the Royal Ballet School in London when she was a teenager?'

Cara frowned. 'Rings a bell.'

'I'm thinking that's the connection with the ballet positions, or at least I was 'til this morning. Duncan is dead and Alec is out for the count. Nobody else knew, nothing was ever leaked, I'm as confident as I can be of that.'

'So in conclusion,' Cara sighed. 'It's all clear as mud.'

'RIGHT MISSUS, enough of this scaring us all half to death.'

Hannah perched at the edge of the gurney and squeezed Jade's hand. Jade could see the worry in her eyes and felt a stab of guilt. The paramedics had stuck her in a corridor and promised she would be transferred to a cubicle as soon as somebody saw her, even as Jade protested and swore blind she was perfectly fine to get up and walk home. Now she had been lying on the gurney, bored out her bonkers, for several hours while harassed medical staff charged by. Now and then somebody offered her tea, but then rushed off before she could answer.

'Ach it's a load of nonsense bringing me in here,' she said with a grin that was only half forced. 'I'm mortified at taking up space when I'm probably healthier than half the staff.'

'You did black out though, that's no good.'

Jade shrugged. 'You know me, never one to do things by halves. It's not common for panic attacks to cause actual faints, but it is possible, fact fans.'

She gave a thumbs up, and only then noticed Hannah's boyfriend Ruari hovering awkwardly in the background.

She had only met Ruari once or twice, during his obligatory *meet the friends* tour when they were first established as a proper couple, but there was a kindness about him she immediately liked. And a way of making Hannah's eyes light up she liked even more.

Other than the Andy years, Jade and Hannah and been single partners-in-crime since they were teenagers. They'd cheerfully waved off most of their school friends into wifedom throughout their twenties, once memorably crashing into each other in their panic to escape a bridal bouquet being lobbed right at them. The bouquet had ended up in a puddle and the bride burst into tears and Jade and Hannah tried desperately to compose their giggles into expressions of appropriate guilt and sorrow.

'How's it possible yous two smashers dave not got men?' some vision in a too-tight kilt whose breath was about 80% proof slurred at them later that night.

'Just lucky, I guess,' grinned Jade and they both fell about in stitches at his baffled expression.

Though they had carefully shied away from ever explicitly discussing it, Jade had always put Hannah's vague dislike of Andy down to the fact that he had taken her pal from her. It was typical that Hannah had got together with Ruari just weeks after Jade split up with Andy, but Jade was a tiny bit pleased with herself that she had never let any such resentment stop her from seeing that Ruari was basically good people. It wasn't as though she needed a wingwoman anyway: until she got her brain back in functional mode, the only romance in her life came via special delivery from Ann Summers.

'Do you know what set it off?' Ruari asked now.

Jade shrugged. 'Fuck knows. The usual shite. Nothing. Everything.' Without warning her eyes filled with tears and she swallowed back a sob as Hannah grabbed her in a hug.

'Aye I do know actually. A guy I know — a pal of mine, I mean, just to say hello to, but still — he was murdered last night. Or this morning, I'm not sure.'

'The guy in the papers?' Hannah asked, trying unsuccessfully to mask the shock in her voice.

Jade nodded. 'It's just — I can't get my head round it. I had clients all day since I heard, so I've not really had a chance to think about it properly. I'm getting way better at controlling the attacks before they really get going, but this one just knocked me for six.'

'Oh no wonder,' Hannah said, hugging her close.

Ruari came a bit closer, leaned against the wall at the foot of the gurney. His arms were crossed and he looked uncomfortable. Too late, Jade remembered that his best friend had been murdered a couple of years ago.

'Sorry,' she said, and he shook his head.

'Not at all.' He smiled sadly. 'I remember that feeling. Grief has a nasty habit of coming at you out of nowhere.'

'Aye but it's not grief, though. I couldn't honestly say that. I went through grief when my gran went. This is — I mean, I'm sad, obviously, he was a lovely guy and I'll miss him, but I can't pretend to be feeling what his friends and family must be. It's just — I don't even know, it's —'

'Too close to home?' Ruari asked gently and Jade shivered. Someone must be walking over her grave.

'Yeah. I mean, no. It's not about me, it's got nothing to do with me. I know that, it's —'

'It's totally understandable it freaked you out, Jade,' Hannah said firmly. 'No, it doesn't have anything to do with you, but you're still dealing with what happened to you. It's no wonder —'

'I don't want to be like this,' Jade blurted. 'I'm so sick of it.'

Hannah squeezed her hand as a smiley nurse appeared pushing a trolley that rattled with various instruments.

'Hello there, Jade McFadyen? I am so sorry you've been stuck here this long, we've had a day and a half of it already and my shift just started. Now if you could just look at my ear here while I shine a wee light in your eyes. Maybe your pals could go and get you a wee cup of tea?'

While the nurse poked and prodded her and generally made sure she wasn't a liability to be set free on the streets, the words *I don't want to be like this* rattled round Jade's head. That was exactly the problem, she realised.

She wasn't like this. Jade was a woman of action. She made stuff happen. She'd bought her flat, started her own business, chatted Andy up, all because she set her mind to it and then she just did it. She was a walking bloody motivational meme.

Except she wasn't any more. She felt like an empty plastic bag drifting in the wind, one of those thin, cheap ones, discarded from somebody's takeaway. She was buffeted this way and that, catching on branches, slammed against walls, with no say over what she thought or knew or felt. Sometimes she would wake up and be fine. Other times she would be furious, terrified, or drowning in heartbreak over that bloody glass cabinet Andy, when in reality she'd reached the 'dodged a bullet' stage long ago.

When the nurse pronounced her fit for purpose, Hannah and Ruari insisted on seeing her home in a taxi. Jade was quiet the whole time, and pretended she didn't notice the concerned looks they exchanged over her head as she half-dosed in the cab against Hannah's shoulder.

In Jade's flat, Hannah ordered Ruari to make tea and

toast while she tucked Jade up on the sofa under her Granny's crocheted throw. 'I don't have the flu,' Jade protested weakly as Hannah fussed around her, though she had a lump in her throat. It had been a while since anybody had looked after her.

'Oh you've burnt the toast, you numpty,' Hannah rolled her eyes affectionately at Ruari. She took the plate from him and hurried back to the kitchen. Ruari handed Jade her tea in her favourite mug.

'Hopefully I didn't burn that as well,' he grinned as Jade took a sip. 'Though knowing me, it's more than possible.'

'It's perfect,' Jade smiled. 'Wasn't there once some daft advert where somebody says something about a lovely cup of tea? That's what this is, a lovely cup of tea. I'm really grateful, but you should both get away up the road home now. I'm not an invalid.'

'Aye, but, listen, before we go. Tell me to get lost if you want,' Ruari said, perching on her coffee table. 'But I might know somebody who could help you.'

4

'*Three wee boys, sat upon a wa'*
Sat upon a wa'a'a
Three wee boys, sat upon a wa'
On a cold and frosty morning.'

'Three wee craws, isn't it no', Ceitidh?' asked Rasmus as he poured tea into a china cup and saucer and set it on the ornate side table next to Ceitidh's armchair. Her chair was facing the large bay window, as usual, and as usual she was staring out over the bay. Today the clouds were dark and low and the waves white-tipped. The hazy outline of the Cuillin mountains brooded on the horizon. A low, threatening rumble of thunder sounded in the distance.

Ceitidh's long white hair was twisted into a neat bun. Her husband arranged for a hairdresser to come to her twice a week, and Ceitidh submitted to the wee lassie's attentions contentedly enough as long as she could still see out her window as the girl combed and twisted. Now, she picked up her tea and took a sip as Rasmus put a couple of ginger biscuits on a plate for her.

'Is that not how the song goes?' he persisted. 'Three wee

craws, sat upon a wa'. It had been a long time since Ceitidh had shown any sign of being aware of his presence, but Rasmus continued to blether away on his tea rounds every morning, just like he did with all the residents.

'Three wee boys,' she muttered again, staring at the low, threatening clouds and holding her tea with surprisingly steady hands. A giant wave crashed against the beach, shooting a white spray high into the murky sky. Rasmus followed Ceitidh's gaze and noticed for the first time that she was staring at the remains of a rocky wall that zig zagged between the rarely used garden and the beach. The wall was crumbling in places and almost engulfed by reeds.

'That wall?' he asked curiously. 'Is that where three wee boys sat?'

Ceitidh reached for the biscuits and crumbled one in her hand.

To the left of the beach, a craggy hill rose sharply overhead. Its summit disappeared into the clouds this morning, but Rasumus didn't need to see the dilapidated old castle that overshadowed the village to know it was there. To Rasmus, it was just an ugly old building, but he knew that everyone in the village hated it. Several petitions had been raised to have it demolished.

'It's an eyesore,' insisted Eunice McBride, a long time resident and undisputed Queen Bee of the day room. 'It should have been got rid of years ago.'

Rasmus didn't think it was just the aesthetics that bothered the village folk. Scotland was full of crumbling old castles, after all. He remembered going a bike ride to a park on the outskirts of his home town of Tallin just a few weeks after the Soviet Union collapsed.

Deep in the woods, he and his best friend Oliver came across a pile of discarded statues of Stalin. They had been

ripped from around the city within hours of Estonia's eman-
cipation. It was bizarre, seeing those imposing statues that
had inspired terror and awe for so many years lying indiffer-
ently on the forest floor, the great man looking pathetic and
comical lying helplessly squint and sometimes even upside
down amongst the moss and the weeds.

'Out of sight, out of mind,' his mother said hours later,
when Rasmus whispered to her what they had found. She
leaned over to kiss him good night. 'If we don't have to see
him every day, it will be easier for us to move forward
without reminders of the past.'

That's what the castle was to the village, Rasmus
thought as he put Ceitidh's empty teacup back on his trolley
and trundled along to the next room. He didn't know what
happened at the castle, but he knew that the villagers did
not want reminded of it. He never asked. Though he had
only been ten when the curtain fell, his childhood ingrained
in him an incuriosity born of survival instinct. All the same,
he always felt there was a lighter feeling in the pub on the
evenings when the clouds were low enough to cloak the
castle.

Out of sight, out of mind.

'On a cold and frosty morning...'

Ceitidh's thin voice followed him out as he knocked on
Eunice's door and braced himself for a tirade of complaints.

CARA HAD DREAMT ABOUT STELLAN. She didn't dream about
him very often. It had happened maybe seven or eight times
since he had been gone, but when she did, the pain was so
acute that she thought her bones would snap with it.

When she was eight or nine, she nicked one of her
mum's magazines, a *Woman* or *Woman's Own*, probably,

because someone at school claimed that it contained some crucial information about this mysterious sex thing everyone kept banging on about. She didn't learn much about the birds and the bees in that particular issue, but she did come across a first person account of a woman who claimed to have woken up in the middle of getting her appendix out.

The article went into gruesome detail about how the woman had become conscious, but because of muscle relaxants had been unable to signal that she was awake and the doctors never knew anything was wrong. She had lain there, trapped and helpless, feeling every excruciating slice of the surgeon's scalpel for hours until the operation was over.

Years later, Cara had a fling with a medical student who told her that was physically impossible, but the image stayed with her. It was how she felt every time she let herself look into the abyss of Stellan's absence. She was being sliced and torn apart from the inside, all the while running incident rooms and ordering coffees and picking up dry cleaning as though her world hadn't shattered.

Those close to her knew fine she'd been a zombie for two years, but a few months ago she had been in the toilet when she overheard a couple of the administrative staff discussing how she didn't seem to care her husband had disappeared. She'd felt perversely pleased with herself. She'd fooled them all.

She sat in her car now, in her usual parking spot outside the station, trying to persuade herself to unclick her seatbelt and go inside and face the world. After twenty-four hours, there would be a mass of witness statements and forensic reports concerning the Bobby O'Brien investigation, waiting for Cara to analyse and evaluate, to tease out loose ends and discrepancies and potential lines of enquiry to assign to her team. She had to make an initial report to Liam, she thought sourly. That could wait until the end of the day.

She needed to make some kind of statement to the media. The media was going nuts over the more gruesome aspects which Cara had hoped to keep contained, both out of compassion for Bobby's family and in the hopes that such details could be used to help evaluate and discard any false witnesses or even false confessions. She had been frustrated though not overly surprised to discover that the literal gory details had been leaked to the press. With the speed and extensiveness of social media reporting, it was next to impossible to control the outpouring of news any more.

There were other ways to sift out the cranks and the time wasters she thought, yawning deeply and unclicking her seatbelt. They'd just have to cross that bridge when they came to it.

'Good morning to you, beautiful girl,' Liam's grin greeted her as she got out the car. Cara's brain couldn't quite rouse itself to remind him she wasn't bloody well beautiful in the workplace, and hadn't been a girl in nearly two decades. She just stared at him until his smile faded.

Liam's Belfast accent hadn't dulled a jot after more than two decades in Glasgow. 'It's because he wants folk to see him as a charming... leprechaun,' Cara once growled to Stellan. Every time he screws someone over, he grins and shrugs like *ahh ye caught me, so you did! What a cheeky scamp I am. Fucking fuckwaffle that he is.*'

Hours later, Stellan had poked her awake to complain he couldn't find *fuckwaffle* in the dictionary.

'Helluva case you've been landed with,' he said, falling into step with her. Liam's dark auburn hair, now more salt than pepper, was still damp from his morning shower and artfully ruffled in a way Cara found intensely irritating.

'Well, that's my job.'

'I know, but I don't want you taking on too much, especially so soon after the last one.'

'I'm fine. What last one?'

'The snafu of the other day'

Cara flinched, realising with a hot flash of guilt that she'd forgotten about the not guilty verdict.

'You handed the procurator fiscal a bloody bang to rights conviction If he was too much of a doddering old fool to see it through, it's not your fault.'

'The jury didn't consider the evidence to be there.'

'Ach what does a fucking jury know about anything? Look Cara, you are doing a grand job despite what you might think, and don't let anyone tell you different. I went over your case before I signed off and there's hardly a thing I'd have done differently.'

'Well I'm glad to hear that.'

They'd reached the door but Cara stopped, sensing she would rather complete this conversation where they were less likely to be overheard.

'Look, Cara,' said Liam. 'Are you okay? Honestly, just between us. Has there been any news on Stellan?'

'I'm — as okay as I ever am. No, there's been no news.'

'I'm worried about you. As an old pal, I've been worried about you for a while. Taking on an investigation like this, with the press attention and all, it's going to be big. I want you to know that you can always come to me if — well the thing is, we all need to be firing on all cylinders.'

Cara stared, stunned for an instant. For a horrible moment she could feel all-too-present tears prickle beneath her eyelids. Then she took a deep breath, looked Liam coldly in the eye. 'I am absolutely fine. If you have a specific example of where my conduct has let the team down, please take it up with me officially.'

'Cara, no, that isn't what I meant, pet. I just — I worded that badly. Forget the investigation, forget the job.' Liam leaned forward and took Cara's hand. 'I'm concerned about you as a friend. I know we've had this conversation before, but nobody would blame you if you took a leave of absence — or even a holiday for goodness sake. You've worked two Christmases in a row, I don't even know the last time you had a proper weekend.' He held up a hand as Cara started to object. 'You need to process what's happened somehow, and you need some time to do that. You need to come to terms with the fact that he's gone.'

Cara nodded sharply, spoke through gritted teeth. 'Well I — I'll take that in the spirit I'm sure it was intended. Thank you, Liam.'

Liam opened the door and gestured for Cara to go ahead. 'For what it's worth, I considered Stellan a good pal. He was a brilliant guy, and I really miss him too.'

NATALIE CLARKE BURST into tears the minute she opened the door to the two detectives. Samira made eyes at Lauren as she introduced them both to Natalie, explained they were investigating Bobby O'Brien's death and asked if they could have a wee word. Lauren knew the eyes meant 'make tea.'

As she put the kettle on and rooted around Natalie's neat wee kitchen for some teabags, it occurred to Lauren that if a male senior officer made tea eyes at her she'd have bristled at being relegated to a domestic role. She couldn't quite make up her mind whether or not how she felt about Samira doing it.

Lauren placed the tea on the coffee table in front of

Natalie, sat on the sofa next to Samira and as unobtrusively as she could, rooted around in her bag for her notebook, Natalie blew her nose and made an obvious effort to pull herself together. She toyed with a lock of platinum blonde hair and Lauren noticed that it was an extension. The thought popped into her mind Natalie was normally dolled up to the eyeballs. She could just see her in her mind's eye, with the full contingent of lashes and contouring and all that stuff that made Lauren look like a wee girl who'd got into her mum's makeup bag.

Natalie's face was bare now. She looked vulnerable and young, her eyes red raw as she wiped them one more time and took a sip of her tea.

'I'm sorry,' she said in a shaky voice. 'I feel daft, I hardly knew him, I don't have any right to grieve. It's just, when I picture him dropping me off the other night —' She took a shuddery breath, seemed for a moment to be about to dissolve into tears again but then she took a deep breath, toyed with the sodden hanky.

'Bobby's eyes went crinkly when he smiled, know the kind I mean? He smiled all the time as well. I really liked him. I was determined to do it right, make him wait the four dates, like they say in that book, you know? I knew I'd be tempted because he's awful lovely, and when he smiled at me I just went wobbly, so before our third date, I never shaved my legs or booked in for a wax. Sure enough, soon as I'd had a wee drink I told him he could come in but that he would need a miner's torch and a compass to find my bits.

'His eyes all crinkled up and he said I was a right wee smasher and he looked forward to coming in the next time.' Natalie took a shaky breath. 'This is a good cup of tea.'

She smiled at Lauren and Lauren flushed guiltily, terrified it was written on her face that she was wondering what book said you were supposed to make men wait four dates.

'How did you meet Bobby?' Samira asked gently, and Natalie smiled, though her eyes filled up again.

'The old fashioned way, can you believe it? I was out dancing with some pals and somehow we ended up at The Shed. Think we raised the median age by about half a century, but Bobby was there with some of his gym crew, and he chatted me up.' Her eyes filled up again. 'He came on with this dead cheesy line about my dress matching his bedroom carpet, or something. I rolled my eyes and told him to get tae, and he was like 'no, no, no I'm gonnae try another one, just hold on.'

'He did one about rearranging the alphabet to put I and U together, and I was like 'are you joking?' Then he said, 'right forget the lines, let's just pretend we've known each other for ages. How's your mum?' I said my mum was dead and he nearly died and I burst out laughing because she's not dead, she's the kind of arsehole who'll outlive us all but a wee fright served him right for such shocking patter.' She finally took a breath and Lauren wondered if she really needed to have written all that down.

'And that was that.' Natalie shrugged. 'He took my number like in the olden days and he phoned the next day and asked me for a drink.'

'How many dates did you have?'

'Three,' Natalie said. She glanced down at her tea and Lauren suspected she was wishing she'd buggered the book and shaved her legs for their third date. 'I just — yous never met him, obviously, so you need to believe me when I say he was the loveliest person you'd ever come across. I didn't need to know him well to know that. You know they folk that just light up a room with their smile?

'And I'm not saying that because I fancied him, I've fancied plenty pure roasters who couldnae light up a room with a torch. Bobby was a special person. And you need to know that because you need to know that it just pure makes no sense somebody would murder him.'

Twenty minutes later, Samira snapped on her seatbelt as Lauren swung the car into heavy traffic on Possil Road. She glanced at her watch. Half five, smack bang in rush hour. It would take them the best part of half an hour back to the station at this rate, she thought. They would have been better off walking.

'Do you think maybe we're looking at it the wrong way round?' she blurted, and Samira looked up with a frown. Lauren cringed. She'd been thinking this since the briefing the day before, but had wanted to get Cara alone to put it to her. Cara may have been the more senior officer, but she was a lot less intimidating than Samira.

'The wrong way round how?' Samira asked, and there was an edge to her voice that made Lauren wish she hadn't opened her big mouth.

'Well, you know how we've been thinking it must have been a personal attack because it doesn't make sense for a killer to choose a massive guy like Bobby as a victim?'

'Turn up here,' Samira said suddenly. 'We can nip through this estate and get onto Great Western Road quicker.'

'But what if that's the point?' Lauren pressed on. 'I mean, serial killers, their whole thing is power, isn't it? They're logical in some ways, but not necessarily practical like you or I would understand practicality. Look at the way somebody like Stuart Henderson used to cut his bodies to pieces, like he was doing a post mortem or something. That must have taken hours when he could have been escaping, not to mention got him all covered in blood and goodness knows what. Anybody thinking rationally about not getting caught would have just taken off, so what if we're missing a trick by thinking in terms of what we see as a logical victim. What if this killer chose Bobby O'Brien *because* he was such a challenge?'

Samira shrugged. 'It would be unusual.'

'What he did to Bobby was unusual.'

'Stuart Henderson spent those hours with his victim's bodies in forests in America in the middle of nowhere. The chances of someone happening upon them were next to none, evidenced by the fact he wasn't caught for over a decade. He was pretty logical.'

'Aye I know, but — I did a project about Vikings at school, and they had this belief that if they killed a warrior in battle they took on his life force. The idea was that if they did that enough they would become immortal, that's one of the reasons they were so fearless in battle, they didn't see it as risking death but as a chance to live forever. Apparently some scholars believe that's where the idea of vampires comes from, that concept of fuelling yourself with someone else's lifeblood.'

'Aye right,' Samira said with a yawn, getting her phone out. 'We'll maybe hold off telling Cara you think there's a Viking-vampire on the streets of Glasgow, eh?'

THE OFFICE WAS in the attic of a once-grand building just off George Square. It now housed several drab offices of almost comically dull companies. Jade wondered if the old building would fall down in panic if a trendy Startup or PR agency moved in, as she humphed up yet another flight of stairs to be greeted with signs welcoming her to stationary supplies and ventilation consultants. The final flight of stairs was so narrow she could only just walk straight without banging her shoulders on the walls.

At the top of the stairs was a the tiny waiting room that should have been cramped but somehow wasn't, thanks to the large skylight windows that bathed it in bright light even on the dullest day. It and office within were decorated in light, calming, vaguely Scandinavian tones of scrubbed pine and whitewashed floors.

Jade sat on a comfy periwinkle blue chair and closed her eyes, grateful for a moment's peace. She couldn't make up her mind if she was dreading what was coming next, or looking forward to it. Worrying away at that awning abyss where her memory should be was a bit like picking at the scab on a nasty cut. She was terrified of the pain that opening the wound would bring, but at the same time it was better than the interminable itch of not knowing.

'Jade? Sorry to keep you waiting.'

Jade looked up and saw a surprisingly small woman, delicate boned and pale, her long red hair tumbling down her back, standing in the doorway. This was the great Dr. Amy Kerr?

Ruari had told her some stuff about Amy Kerr the night before when he texted to make Jade an appointment the following day. As soon as he and Hannah left, Jade looked Amy up and spent much of the night clicking through pages and pages of results, skimming articles about the husband on death row and how she had been kidnapped by the Dancing Girls Killer, before escaping and killing another of Alec McAvoy's puppets who tried to attack her.

She was dressed like a normal person, Jade noticed. She liked that. Her first therapist, the patronising git, had worn a suit, which made Jade feel as though she were meeting a parole officer. The second therapist's hippy dippy numbers had put Jade on edge, worried she might start chanting and sprinkling flowery water to cleanse her aura or something.

Dr Kerr wore black jeans, a denim shirt and an ancient pair of DMs, not a million miles from Jade's own jeans, knitted jumper and biker boots. Jade wondered if she was in casual dress because it was Saturday or if this was her usual garb. Either way, she immediately felt at ease.

'Can I ask a question?' she asked when Dr Kerr curled up in her armchair facing the sofa and picked up her notebook and pen. Jade perched at the edge of the sofa, her hands clasped as she stared at the knots in the wood of the sturdy oak coffee table in front of her. She felt the abyss beckoning, and suddenly wanted nothing more than to walk out and run all the way home.

'Is it about you or me?' Dr Kerr asked gently, and Jade was grateful that she didn't pretend.

'You.'

'Fair enough. We're not here to talk about me, but I'll do you a deal. You get to ask three questions, anything you like, and I promise to answer them fully and honestly. Then that's the last we talk about me. Deal?'

Jade nodded. 'Do you miss your husband?' she asked, though that wasn't what she had been planning to ask.

'Yes. I miss who I thought he was. The man I lived with for ten years, who made me cheese on toast if I had a cold and gave me all his socks. If I was moaning about my PHD supervisor or some wee annoying thing that happened at the shops, he would get up and start doing the running man until I laughed. I miss him. I miss him a lot.'

'Does it count as a second question if I ask if giving you all his socks is a euphemism?'

Amy smiled. 'No, I'll give you that one. When we first

started going out, we were out for a walk one day, and he told me that he would give me anything I wanted to make me happy. I think I was supposed to think in terms of the moon and the stars or some romantic nonsense, but for whatever daft reason, I blurted out 'can I have all your socks?' So he posted me all his socks in a great big box.' She chuckled, shook her head. 'That was Stuart for you.'

'Were you scared of him?'

Amy thought about this for a moment. 'Have you ever stepped off a boat or something and nearly went flying because the ground wasn't moving any more? You hadn't felt wobbly on the boat because your body just adapted and absorbed it, but when it was gone your body didn't know what to do with itself any more?'

Jade nodded. She felt tense, all of a sudden, though it didn't make sense. They were talking about Amy, not her. She forced herself to take a breath, to let her shoulders drop.

'It was a bit like that. I lived with Stuart for eleven years, and for most of that time I would have told you we were happy. We rarely fought. He was never cruel, never nasty. Like I said, he made me cheese on toast, made me laugh. Yet once he was gone, I nearly fell over from the relief.

'The morning he was arrested, I was in the bath and I had started to slit my wrists. The FBI ran in right in the middle of it, and at first they thought he must have stabbed me before he left. I had to correct them.' Amy shook her head. 'I ended up offering them the receipt for the scalpel from my purse to prove I had bought it myself. If there's a more awkward conversation than that I'd like to know what it is.'

Jade stared at her, a heavy feeling unfurling in her stomach.

'At the time I couldn't even have told you why. Even given

the circumstances, it still took me years to make the connection between how Stuart made me feel and how I ended up in that bath that morning.'

'And you're a psychologist.'

'I promise I'm better when it comes to treating other people.'

Jade smiled. 'I'm not sure I'm treatable.'

'Why not?'

Jade shrugged and was annoyed to notice she was close to tears. *Pull yourself together,* she thought. They hadn't even started yet. 'Because I already do all the stuff,' she sighed. 'I journal, I breathe, I salute the sun on a regular basis. It's rational and normal to be scared after someone tried to kill me, I know that. I get it, I accept it.

'Plus it happened right after my gran died — she raised me, she was the only family I had. And just for good measure, it the day after my bloody boyfriend of four years finished with me. I had a shite time. I'm not in denial, I'm not phobic about the attacks, I crack on with my life as best I can and I manage them when I have to.'

'So why do you think they're still coming?'

'I don't fucking know,' Jade snapped. 'It doesn't make any sense. That's the problem. That's why I'm here on a Saturday morning when I could be having a lie-in.'

Why had she bothered with this, she wondered angrily. Bloody Ruari, claiming his pal could help her when no one else could. It was a waste of time. She should have known better. Should have told Ruari not to bother himself sticking his nose in. He'd got her in a weak moment, with all his making her a good cup of tea patter. Shitebag.

'Do you go back to the morning after the attack in your mind, every time?' Amy asked.

'No. Just — I don't know, one out of every three or four ?

My theory is that the terror comes and my brain looks for a reason for it, and the only reason it can come up with is that the attack only just happened.

'My friend Hannah — Ruari's girlfriend — hates flying, and every time we've taken a flight together, she's been convinced she hears the plane making a funny noise, or that the turbulence isn't normal turbulence but shaking that indicates the plane stalling or something. We went to Tuscany a few years ago, and she was having kittens over this hissing noise, certain the plane had sprung some kind of leak, and it turned out to be the coffee pot. She knows fine what a coffee pot sounds like, she was a barista for years, but I think brains lock onto logical reasons to be scared so as to feed the fear.' Jade shrugged. 'That's my theory, anyway.'

'That makes a lot of sense. You've obviously given this a lot of thought. Have you considered hypnosis at all? It can have great results with recovering lost memories.'

Fear had clutched at Jade with such intensity that it nearly took her breath away. She flinched, shook her head. 'No. No, absolutely not.' The thought of not being in control, of lying on a couch, dozy and compliant and unprepared, filled her with such pure terror that for a moment she thought she would be sick.

'I understand it's a scary prospect,' Amy said gently, 'and I promise we would go as slowly and as cautiously as you need to. But I believe that recovering your memory of what happened that night will prove crucial to your recovery. Your theory of your mind looking for a rational reason for fear makes sense, but I also think it's worth considering that your mind keeps catapulting you back to that time because it's trying to tell you something. Like Lassie or something, whining and tugging you into a collapsed cave because there is a child trapped there.'

'I'm not a child,' Jade snapped, though Amy hadn't said she was.

'Just keep it in mind as a possibility.'

Jade nodded tightly, though there was no chance she would consider hypnosis. She would recover the memories consciously, she promised herself. Somehow.

'I never asked my third question,' she said.

'Go ahead.'

'Do you ever regret killing the man who attacked you that night?'

'Never,' Amy said firmly.

'Will I see you next week, then?'

HE SAT on a bench in George Square, his hands deep in his pockets, as the clouds came in to obliterate the sun and a chilly wind snaked its way under his collar. He didn't feel the cold. He didn't feel anything. He didn't know how long he had been sitting there. Minutes, hours. It didn't matter. Nothing mattered except what he was going to do next.

People scurried past. A group of kids who looked like they hadn't been home from last night's dancing yet passed a bottle of Irn Bru between them on the grass in front of him. A young dad shoogled a buggy absentmindedly as he read something on his phone. Tourists milled about, taking photos of the statues, Queen Street station, the inane sign behind him claiming that people made Glasgow.

People didn't make Glasgow, he thought with a smile. That was just something the powers-that-be told folk so they felt important and didn't revolt when they were shunted into yet another council flat that should have been condemned years ago.

'Don't worry your wee head about asbestos and black mould and twenty flights of stairs when the lift packs in again, oh and by the way we're cutting your benefits — you make Glasgow! Congratulations.'

Power made Glasgow. Chaos made Glasgow. No one knew that better than him.

The papers were obsessed. A warm glow of satisfaction prickled over him as he thought over the headlines he had memorised. For days, they had picked over every minute detail of the first one, like pathetic, starving dogs over scraps on a bone. Especially the mutilation. He might have known the prurient wee buggers would go mental for that.

Of course, if people weren't so stupid he wouldn't need to be doing this at all. That was what pissed him off. He wasn't some bloodthirsty psychopath driven by a primal need for violence. He would have been quite happy just to live a normal life. The problem was, the world was so fucked up in a way that only he understood and therefore only he could fix, and that was just the cross he had to bear.

He closed his eyes, excitement and terror and dread all churning as one deep inside him. What if he stopped now? What if he just went home to his flat and ordered a pizza and watched a film on Netflix? But even as he pictured dropping off in front of the telly, half a beer dangling from his hand, he knew he would do what he had to.

Bobby O'Brien had offered to help what he thought was an old codger struggling with an injured dog in Victoria Park. Then Bobby O'Brien was gone. It had all gone like clockwork, as he knew it would.

He had been sick when he broke the dog's leg, he remembered. He had found hurting the dog harder than what came next.

Afterward it was all finished, he drove the dog to Helensburgh and shoved it in the water where it whimpered as it hit

*the waves and he realised it hadn't been dead after all, just
stunned.*

*He had thought about jumping in to save it. He could pretend
he had just found it in the water. He could take it to a vet like a
Good Samaritan, exchange horrified speculation as to what kind
of monster would try to drown an injured animal. But just as he
was about to jump in, a cold wind blew up and he realised how
freezing the water would be.*

*Chances were the dog had died of shock in the past few
seconds anyway. It was a shame, but what was done was done.*

CARA HANDED Ruari a bottle of lager then padded out to the
paved patio. Her garden was small, bordered by a high wall
that was strewn with a mass of creeping wildflowers. The
night air was chilly, but scented with something flowery
Ruari was sure Hannah would be able to identify. All he
knew was that it was nice.

'It's like the secret garden out here,' he said as he sat on
the wicker loveseat. Cara was curled in a swinging armchair
wrapped in a chenille throw. There was a matching swing
opposite her, but Ruari suspected it was Stellan's so he stuck
to the loveseat. The sky was still brilliant white, but the light
was almost gone and Ruari could only just make out the
shape of Cara in the shadows as she sipped her beer in
silence.

'The first time I went to Stockholm,' she said suddenly,
and Ruari nearly jumped a mile. 'It wasn't long after Christmas, mid January or so. They still had all their Christmas
lights up. They keep them up until the end of January, but
my mum had a thing about how you have to take them
down before Hogmany or you get bad luck for the year. I've
never been superstitious, but I remember finding it stressful

seeing all the lights twinkling all over the city.' She smiled, and Ruari heard the catch in her breath as she remembered.

'I'd never felt cold like it in my life,' she said. 'There were these giant piles of snow and ice on every street corner where they'd been cleared by these huge machines and you could get an ice cream headache just from breathing. I nearly died when I saw folk sitting outside every wee café or coffee shop, wrapped up in blankets. Stellan said they did that year round, even in the heaviest snow. They're a bit obsessed with fresh air.'

'It is nice being outside,' Ruari said, though in fact he was freezing. It was quiet up here in Cara's leafy suburb. He could hear the wails of a baby from somewhere down the road, and a taxi rumbled to a stop nearby.

'You know what someone said to me the other day? One of my mum's neighbours, she caught me on the way back to my car last Sunday. She said it would be easier if I knew he was dead. Then at least I could grieve.'

'Did you nut her?' Ruari asked, and was rewarded with a ghost of a smile.

'Then she started going on about how Sweden has the highest rate of suicide in the world. I snapped that that was a myth, though in fact I haven't a clue. Then just as I was getting into the car, she added that he "most likely" hadn't just run off with someone his own age.'

'That was some hat trick.'

'The funny thing is, I could live with it if he'd gone off with some wee lassie. It would hurt, sure, but I've never believed that partners are possessions or in any till death us do part bollocks. I'd never have wanted him to stay with me if he was so much as thinking about other women. I'd have been sad, but I would have known that our story had come to an end.' She sighed. 'But the thing is, I know Stellan. I know, without a shadow of doubt, that if he wanted out of our marriage, he would have sat me down and had a respectful conversation about it. I'd have called him a fanny and told him to wynch someone else in front of me like a man.'

'I've never done that,' said Ruari in surprise.

'No, I don't expect you have either. But you're a wee one-off, Ruari. ' She smiled ruefully. 'You both are.'

'I should go,' Ruari said, putting his beer bottle on the glass coffee table. 'But I've got two more sightings to check out, one in Italy, the other in England somewhere. Then I'm going to look into —'

'Then maybe it's time you give up.' Cara spoke in the same light tone, but there was an edge to her voice that sent a shiver down Ruari's spine. 'Accept he's gone.'

'No,' he said. 'Definitely not.'

He felt rather than saw Cara's shrug. 'Suit yourself.'

He got up. 'I'm gonnae get us another couple of beers, and then I'll show you the email from the woman in Italy. Her description is good, I think it's promising.'

Cara didn't respond, but he went into the kitchen anyway. As he rooted around the cutlery drawer for a bottle opener, he realised that his heart was pounding.

Though he hadn't broached the subject with Cara, the truth was, Stellan hadn't been seen or heard from for several hours by the time Ruari caught sight of McAvoy in the Lismore that evening they tried to corner him. Ruari knew that Stellan and Cara had exchanged a handful of texts around lunchtime that day, but after that, Cara had been caught up in preparing for the arrest. She hadn't been in touch with him again.

McAvoy could have disposed of Stellan before he went to track Ruari and Jen down. And unless he ever woke up, they would never know. Ruari carried the beers in one hand as he pulled his phone out with the other. He'd text Hannah and say he was going to kip here. She would understand.

When he got back outside, Cara hadn't moved.

EVERY ONCE IN A WHILE, it occurred to Amy to wonder what Stuart would think if he could see her now. She thought it when she was out for drinks with Moira and her crew, screaming with laughter as they chatted up some blushing wee barman who was young enough to be one of their sons. She thought about it when she spent an entire Saturday afternoon cooking in contented solitude, listening to an eclectic mix of country and funk rock and cheesy pop that would have driven any other human stark raving mad, rolling out dough for fresh pasta and slicing tomatoes straight from her lovingly tended-to plant. And she thought about it when she went running.

She had started running after Greer's conviction. Right up until the last minute, they had all been convinced that, somehow, the procurator fiscal would be convinced that there was no case to answer. Alec McAvoy had ordered Greer's sister's murder. And then he had laughed when Cara admitted that there may not be a crime to charge him with.

Amy shuddered as she jogged on the spot, waiting for the green man at Partick Cross. It was one of those nondescript, in between seasons days. Neither hot nor cold, sunny nor dull. Clouds scudded by, though the sky beyond was a friendly blue that promised there just might be a summer this year. McAvoy's laugh had been gleeful that night in the half demolished building. Lorna was nothing but a game he had won; a pawn he had stolen through cunning.

Though Ruari had been heartsick at Greer having to live

with McAvoy's injuries on her conscience, Amy suspected that letting that laugh go unpunished would have festered on Greer's soul, ultimately causing more damage than her eighteen month stretch. Even so, the evening after Greer was sentenced, Amy found herself stepping out of her flat and breaking into a run.

She was far from kitted out that day, in battered old sandshoes and no sports bra. At one point she thought she was going to take out half a bus queue with an errant boob, and after going over on her ankle in Kelvingrove Park, she'd limped home, breathless, with a stitch, throbbing feet and an inexplicable sore elbow. All the same, she was addicted.

For the first time since the FBI banged on her front door that morning, she was thinking of nothing but how much she hated running. No Stuart, no Alec, no Lorna or Kelly or Davie or Paige. Just running and hating running. It was the sweetest relief she could remember in a long time. She went out that day and bought herself some proper trainers and a decent sports bra, Ever since, she had treated herself every couple of days to the respite of an hour raging at herself for being the kind of fanny who goes for a run on purpose.

Stuart would laugh his face off at her, huffing and puffing and scowling her way along the pavement, she thought as she headed down to the Clyde walkway and melted in with the early evening joggers and cyclists. Though Amy vaguely recalled strict rules separating bikes from pedestrians from her time in the States, in most of Glasgow it was heart-stopping free-for-all in which one wrong footstep would get you on the receiving end of a furious bell tinkle and weirdly mute roar of abuse when the cyclist's fury was stolen by the wind as they zipped by in a fit of pique.

'I don't know what it is about getting on a bike that

makes some folk perpetually furious,' Amy had shrugged to Moira when she popped round bearing a bottle of rosé and a double portion of chips the other night.

'Ach if I was cutting about with one of those wee seats up my jacksy I'd be in the huff too,' Moira replied with a grimace, refilling both their glasses. 'Cannae be good for a person.'

It was a coincidence that she was running in Victoria Park last week when that poor bugger was found, Amy repeated to herself for the millionth time. If she'd not slowed down to check that the wee girl in the glittery dress was okay, she would have seen the body before the dog walker started screaming, but it was just rotten luck. The body could have been left in any park in the city; she could have chosen to run in any park in the city.

It was just a coincidence.

There must be a gig or something on at the SECC she realised with dismay as she bounded up the stairs of the footbridge across the motorway two at a time. The car park was full, and crawling with folk decked in a copious amounts of hot pink and glitter. Excited shrieks filled the air.

A teeny bopper concert, Amy thought with a grin, remembering her mum taking her and a couple of pals from school to see Jason Donovan sometime in the dim and distant past. She had worn a T shirt with a picture of the *Especially for You* single cover on it, and on the train on the way in to town some bigger girls informed her that Kylie had just dumped Jason for Michael Hutchence.

Amy was horrified, convinced that if Jason looked out into the crowd and saw his ex-girlfriend on her T shirt, it would upset him and ruin his whole night. Even though her mum kept trying to explain that it really wasn't likely he would spot her, and probably he was okay, it took two to end a relationship, Amy went into the toilets as soon as they arrived and turned her T shirt inside out. Her mum bought her a glo-stick to make her feel better. She waved it during *Any Dream Will Do* and was 99% certain he saw her then, and it didn't ruin his night.

There was no point in trying to shove her way through those crowds, Amy thought now, skipping back down the stairs. She'd loop up past Kelvin Hall and through the park a bit, and that would just have to do.

Even with the wee detour, she was still barely out of breath when she fumbled in her inside pocket for the wee key to her tenement's front door. The front door flew open and she was nearly barrelled to the ground by a young guy in a leather jacket who ran into the road as though he was on fire. He was a good-looking boy, Amy thought as she grabbed the door before it swung shut. Tall and slim with hip bones you could get a paper cut from, he put Amy in mind of the emaciated indie bands of her post-Jason Donovan years.

Something about his face rang a vague bell, though she couldn't quite place him. Must be one of her neighbour's gentlemen callers, she decided. Somebody on the floor above Amy seemed to be holding an ongoing parade of sheepish males trooping meekly through the close on weekend mornings. More than once, Amy had had to do the awkward 'no, no, you first' dance with a mildly shell-shocked boy when she nipped out for milk in her jammies.

Amy wasn't sure what it was about her front door that alerted her. She tended to leave the storm doors open during the day, and one was ajar, but that wasn't it. The postman often pulled one over to stick a package behind it.

It wasn't the postman, she thought, as she crept slowly up the last couple of stairs, every nerve jangling to attention.

There it was. On the mat, slightly behind the storm door. A small, dark thing Amy couldn't for the life of her identify.

Then she stepped forward and saw it clearly and felt a physical slam of terror that made her blood run icy and her breath catch in her throat.

It was a pair of socks.

5

'Scuse me — hello? Sorry to bother you.'

Scott Myers was just pulling his goggles down over his eyes when he caught sight of the woman waving at him from the paddleboard, a few metres from the shore. The wee beach at Balmaha was quiet at this hour. Loch Lomond was as still as glass, reflecting the deep blue of the early morning sky.

'I couldn't ask a favour could I? Sorry to be a pain.'

'No problem,' Scott smiled. There weren't many women who could pull off a wetsuit, but this one, with her short, light brown hair and sporty figure, was definitely giving it a college try.

'Oh are you American?' she asked in surprise.

'I'm Canadian,' he replied with an easy grin. 'But pretty close. I'm from White Rock, BC. You can see the US border from my parents' house.'

'Oh... very good,' she said with a slightly nonplussed smile.

'How can I help?'

'Oh god, I'm such a tube. My paddle went and broke the

minute I got out here and it's sunk. It's no' even that deep here, but I've got contacts in and I'll never find it with my eyes shut. Seeing as you've got goggles, would you mind —'

'Sure, no problem at all.'

Scott pulled his goggles down, waded into the bracing water and nimbly dove beneath her board. Even with his goggles on, visibility was low. The thick mass of deep green vegetation seemed to suck all the light so that just a metre or two down, it was as dark as night. He felt around for anything that resembled a paddle for a few seconds before he had to surface for a breath with an apologetic smile.

'Let me try again,' he breathed.

When he surfaced for the third time, the woman begged him not to bother again. 'It must have drifted away already, or got tangled in some reeds. What an arse, but we're not far out, I can swim in dragging the board.'

'Are you sure? It's no problem to try a while longer?'

'Honestly, I feel bad. You get on with your swim. I'm going to hang around for a while seeing as I'm missing out on my paddle, maybe when you get back I could buy you a beer to say thanks for trying?'

Scott raised an eyebrow. Well, okay then. It was taking him a while to get used to these Scottish women who hadn't gotten the 'hard to get' memo, but he definitely wasn't complaining.

'Sounds like a pretty good plan,' he smiled lazily, enjoying the way she blushed as though she couldn't quite believe her nerve. 'In fact, if I beat last week's time we can follow it up with a whisky to celebrate.'

'Then you'd better get going.'

JADE's gran nearly had a hairy canary when they started

opening cafés that served things like smoked salmon in the East End, and swore she would never be so disrespectful as to sip a soy latte in the shadow of the Necropolis.

'Your granda will rise and haunt me if he gets a whiff of any non-dairy shite,' she declared. 'And if I see that crabbit fucker cutting about above ground, I'll kill him.'

As she sat at a pavement table outside her favourite café on Duke Street waiting for her breakfast, Jade could just picture Granny's wee face screwed up with fury. The closest Gran ever had to her five-a-day was the odd Jaffa cake, but when she took the heart attack that killed her at ninety-three she was in the middle of the keep-fit class she had attended with her pals every week since they retired over thirty years previously. They all sat on chairs and waved their arms about to big band music, killing themselves laughing and stopping to gossip every five minutes, while the wee lassie employed to take the class implored them to please pay just a wee bit of attention.

Gran had left her teeth at home that morning as she often did, because they were stained blue from her session the night before with Jeannie. Her final words were snapping at the wee paramedic to mind his own bloody business when he asked if she normally wore her teeth. Whenever any of Jade's clients muttered about clean eating or started taking counting macros to extremes, Jade would tell them about her Gran and remind them that life was for living.

Jade's hair was still wet from her shower after Bikram yoga. She closed her eyes, enjoying the warmth of the sun on her face. Though she was loathe to admit it, the session with Amy had calmed her. She felt as though she had been clinging to the edge of a cliff in a raging storm for two years. She fully expected the fall to kill her, but on the other hand, the relief of letting go was seductive.

'Are you doing that meditating?'

Jade opened her eyes with a start. Her first thought was that bangers who think it's okay to disturb a woman's peace whenever they fancy it, aren't normally so handsome. The man at the next table was a bit older than her. He had that rakish, *I've seen some stuff,* thing going on, with shaggy salt-and-pepper hair, a deep tan and piercing blue eyes. He was slim, but when he reached for his coffee she noticed the sharp definition in his forearms.

'Sorry, shite,' he added with a sheepish grin. 'If you're at the meditating, you'll be wanting peace.'

'And yet here you are.'

He had a slight accent she couldn't quite place. Highlands? Islands? There was a cadence to his voice that was vaguely singsongy.

'I apologise for disturbing you. I just keep hearing about this meditating lark and I was so fascinated to see someone doing it in real life that I spoke up without thinking. It was rude.'

'It's okay,' Jade shrugged. His expression was so earnest that she felt churlish. 'I wasn't really meditating, I just had my eyes shut.'

'Catching a cheeky wee snooze in the sun?'

'Something like that. I've just been to yoga.'

'So do you know about meditating?'

'A bit. I'm no expert.'

'I don't even know why I'm interested, I don't really get stressed out.' He grinned, squinting slightly in the sun. Something about him reminded Jade of a wizened prairie dog roaming barren wastelands, existing on scraps and scuffles.

'To me, that's a bit like saying I don't have cancer so why do I need to eat fruit and veg,' she said. 'Mental health is worth looking after.' That was rich, coming from her, she thought with a rueful grin.

'Is that right?'

He had an intense gaze, and Jade suddenly felt as though she were under a microscope. She shrugged. 'I think so. But you do you.'

The waitress brought her breakfast out and Jade busied herself buttering the toast, hyper aware of his scrutiny and unable to decide whether or not it made her uncomfortable.

'I like to get the butter on quickly so the toast is still hot enough to melt it too.' he commented, watching her. Then with a brief smile he turned away and picked up his newspaper. Jade felt an absurd flash of disappointment and was immediately annoyed with herself. Hadn't she just been irritated at him interrupting her? She tucked into her breakfast.

'Do you not get ants in your pants having to sit still for that long?' the man asked suddenly, and Jade jumped a mile. 'When you're meditating. I don't think I could keep at peace for long.'

Jade swallowed. 'To begin with it's hard. It takes a bit of practice, but you don't have to do it for a long time until you're ready. Even a few minutes a day is a good start.'

'Maybe you could teach me?'

Jade's stomach twisted. Pins and needles darted into her fingers. 'There are classes you can take,' she muttered.

'Sorry. Again,' he smiled, holding his hands up in surrender. 'Please don't think I'm a nutter. I've been abroad for years, the States.' That explained the funny accent. 'I always forget it terrifies British people if you suggest being mates in five minutes. I'm sorry. I won't bother you again.'

Jade poured her tea, bracing the pot against the side of the mug so her hand didn't tremble. 'It's just that a qualified instructor could teach you better than me,' she said.

'So you do want to be mates?' he grinned, and Jade smiled despite herself. 'I'm Roddy, by the way.'

BOBBY O'BRIEN'S funeral was well attended. His family had been parishioners at St Theresa's in Possilpark for several generations, and it seemed that half of the North of Glasgow had turned out to send him off.

'Spotting a suspicious character in this crowd is gonnae be like picking out a baby swan in a crowd of ducks,' Kevin McGregor muttered as they stood unobtrusively by the front steps of the church, watching the hoards file in.

'What?' Samira demanded with a frown. 'Swans look nothing like ducks.'

'Baby ones do,' Kevin insisted. 'They're brown and fluffy.'

'Ducks aren't fluffy.'

'Baby ones are.' Kevin heard Lauren McNab stifle a snigger as he finally cracked a grin and Samira rolled her eyes.

'I did time at Springburn station when I first qualified,' she muttered. 'I've had the pleasure of half this shower already.'

'Aye, that's my point.'

'Swans still dinnae look like ducks,' she snapped. 'I'm going in. There could be something to the organised crime theory after all.'

'Naw there's not,' Kevin said quietly when Samira had gone. 'She knows that fine.'

As the priest started to give the eulogy a little while later, Kevin caught a movement out of the corner of his eye. Someone had shifted slightly on the pew to Kevin's far right, a row or two in front. He watched carefully, trying to figure out just who had moved. Was it that woman with steel grey hair in a blue coat and old fashioned hat, sobbing softly into a hanky? The huge bald man with his head bent? Or one of those wee girls with long blonde hair in neat plaits, sitting in preternatural silence on the laps of their parents?

The last funeral mass Kevin had been to was for a sister-in-law of his granda's, who had converted when she married and ended up being the most devout of the lot after she was widowed young. Though he found the pomp and ceremony faintly absurd, the priest was kind and Kevin could see the genuine grief of the congregation, deeper than that of the handful of distant relatives who'd shown up out of duty. He realised that he understood a tiny bit the comfort folk like his great-auntie found in the community of religion and felt oddly relieved to finally get it.

'What eye has not seen, and ear has not heard,
and what has not entered the human heart...'

The woman in the blue coat had stepped up to the altar and was giving a reading in a clear, thin voice that trembled slightly. Lauren caught Kevin's eye and he shuddered, wondering if the woman in the blue coat knew what had happened to Bobby's eyes and ears.

Something about the mutilation troubled Kevin, though he couldn't quite put his finger on what it was. It had occurred post mortem, so torture hadn't been a factor. Mutilation could be related to a craving for power, he remembered from his training. The ultimate possession of a human being, beyond taking their life -- taking their humanity too. Still though, Kevin couldn't shake the nagging feeling that they were missing something about why the killer had taken Bobby's face with him.

The night before, Kevin had opened up the pathologist's photos of Bobby's face and forced himself to stare at each one for several minutes, determined to spot what it was that was bothering him. It was to do with the lack of anger, he had thought finally. Despite the violence, this hadn't been a frenzied attack. The neck incisions were deliberate, dispassionate, almost surgical in nature. They spoke to something other than a twisted craving for a gruesome trophy.

'For the spirit scrutinises everything, even the depths of God.'

There was a murmured response and the woman scuttled back to her pew, her face crumpling with tears.

Kevin thought about the insight he had gained taking part in Alec McAvoy's macabre role plays. He remembered the sensation of the world narrowing to him and his prey. That sense of waiting, calculating, planning. Considering and rejecting strategies as to when and how and where to pounce. Analysing the risks, managing the threats.

What if that was it? The thought came to him so suddenly Kevin nearly gasped aloud, and belatedly noticed that everyone else had shuffled on to their knees. He slipped down to the knee rest and bowed his head, his mind racing.

The central mystery in Bobby's death was how on earth someone of his strength was overpowered. There was no trace of sedative in his blood. Blood pooling in the body confirmed that he had been killed more or less where he was found, in an open park with any number of ways to escape. There were no rope burns or any markings suggesting he had been restrained — but what if that was it? If there had been any such markings on his face and neck they would be gone now.

The priest rang a bell and everyone got to their feet. Kevin noticed a man on the other side of the church, a couple of people along from the woman with the blue coat. Now that they were standing, he could see that the man was a head and shoulders taller than most of the congregation, though his head was bent low.

Kevin could only see the back of his head, his bony shoulders encased in a cheap leather jacket, but something about him caught his attention. Was he a wannabe criminal Kevin had hauled into the back of a car when he was in uniform, or a cute boy Kevin had woken up with in what he referred to as his 'lively period' just before he met Jack? Neither rang a bell, he thought as he took in the man's chestnut curls and wracked his brains as to where he had seen them before.

He'd find out his name, maybe get Lauren to have a wee word just to check. Chances were they'd shared an awkward breakfast, he thought with a shrug as the pallbearers lifted the coffin and solemnly proceeded up the aisle. Lithe and unkempt had been just his type, once upon a time.

'WHAT WILL you do if you can't find Stellan, Ruari?' Hannah asked. Her words were nearly stolen by the wind as they stopped on the buff overlooking Loch Lomond, half way up Conic Hill. They'd been climbing at a fair old clip and Ruari felt pleasantly puffed as he stared out over the slate-grey waters of the loch and felt the wind whip up his hood. Hannah sat down on the grass and rummaged in her back-pack for her water bottle. After a moment, Ruari sat next to her.

'I will,' he muttered.

'I — I know you will do everything in your power, and I know you are good at what you do,' she said quietly, 'but you are just one person, Ru. The full might of the police searched for Stellan for months and months, and they've got access to — I don't know, systems, databases. DNA. Cara knows that better than anyone. She can't possibly expect —'

'She doesn't,' Ruari said. 'She doesn't expect me to find him. She hired me because if there's no one looking for him then all hope is lost, not because she thinks I'll find him.' He sighed deeply. 'But I have to find him. Not just for Cara's sake. It's for — for Lorna, for Greer, for me. It won't be finished until Stellan is found.'

Hannah scooted closer to him, put her arm around him and rubbed his back as he talked.

'Stellan disappeared because we caught McAvoy. I'm sure of that. It's too — I mean, it was like clockwork. McAvoy goes down, and Stellan disappears.'

'No closer to the edge!' a harassed mum screeched as three lanky pre-teen boys shoved one another on the grass in front of them. 'If yous go flying aff this bloody hill I'm not going after you!'

'Did McAvoy kill Stellan?' Hannah asked bluntly. 'Is that what you think? Are you looking for a body?'

'I don't know. It makes the most sense. Where has he been all this time if he is alive?'

'But you don't believe it.'

Ruari shook his head. 'Every time I tell myself he must have killed Stellan, my brain just rejects it. It won't take. I know it could be denial, but — but I don't think he's dead. My gut feeling is that, somehow, somewhere, Stellan is alive.'

'Held captive like Amy was on that island?'

Ruari shrugged. 'I think so.'

'He couldn't easily have been taken abroad without passports. Even if they could have got round passport control somehow, how would they force him? They couldn't have exactly marched him onto a ship or lorry at gunpoint without anyone seeing.'

'I've thought about that,' Ruari said. Hannah handed him her water bottle and he took a sip. The clouds parted and a brilliant ray of sunshine sparkled on the loch far below. 'We know that McAvoy exerted some kind of control over his puppets to make them kill for him. He tried to do it to me, making me dependent on him then making me doubt my own reality, that's obviously how he lays the foundations.

'Over the past couple of years I've read everything I can get my hands on about mind control, and it's really scary. The brain's a computer at the end of the day, right? That means it's vulnerable to all sorts of commands we're not consciously aware of. We all do it all the time, whether it's peer pressure or normalising extreme political views, or just making someone think what you want them to do is their idea. McAvoy just took that to the extreme, tapped into his puppets vulnerabilities and exploited them. What if he taught his tricks to someone and they controlled Stellan to come with them, hide away with them?'

'But doesn't the puppet have to be vulnerable in the first place? All the people McAvoy actually got to kill for them weren't exactly shining beacons of positive mental energy.'

'Yeah I guess it's easier or harder with different personalities, but one of the things I read is that there is nothing every one of us isn't capable of given the right circumstances. I didn't really know Stellan well, and I wouldn't have called him vulnerable as such, but he's kind, he's a people pleaser.

'He's the type that would have ended up taking three different girls to a dance at school because he couldn't bring himself to turn any of them down, you know? Or it could have been as simple as them telling him that they've got Cara and they'll hurt her if he doesn't do as they say. That's pretty powerful.'

'Have you had any hallucinations?'

Ruari flinched. 'No. Not in ages.'

He could feel her concerned eyes on him, sensed her disbelief.

'I'm just worried that this stress —'

'I'm not stressed.'

'Aye, I know, but —'

Ruari got to his feet and stretched. 'Let's get going,' he said. 'That cloud looks ominous.'

'Ruari, I'm just trying to —'

'I've had one. In months. That's — that's nothing. And it was barely anything. I was just tired.'

'Since you took on Stellan's case?'

'What does that matter?'

She didn't answer and Ruari sighed, reached for her hand. 'I'm fine. I promise I'm fine.'

AN HOUR LATER, a heavy drizzle was underway as they emerged from the woods back into Balmaha car park hand-in-hand. The small bus was just pulling up to the stop and Hannah tugged Ruari's hand as she started to run for it, but Ruari had glimpsed the blue flashing lights across the road and dread pooled in his stomach.

Hannah followed his gaze. 'It could be a wee fender bender or something,' she said. 'Let's just get on the bus.'

Ruari crossed the road and approached the edge of the crime scene, barely aware of Hannah reluctantly following. A crowd of rubberneckers had gathered at the perimeter of the beach. Two grim-faced constables held them back as a third held the tape up for Cara to duck under.

'This rain will be murder for any forensic evidence,' Ruari murmured.

As he watched, a grim-faced Alison Crawford, other-worldly in her white SOCO suit, greeted Cara. He spotted Samira approaching, and at the other end of the beach Kevin was deep in conversation with a younger woman Ruari didn't know. A couple of Alison's team were scurrying across the beach carrying a white tent. Bright flashes from a technician's camera disturbed the gloom.

The sand around the body was deep red, sodden with blood.

It was a man, Ruari noted with surprise, then remembered the news stories of that poor bastard found in Victoria Park. *That's two*, he thought as a chill seeped into his bones.

The victim was big, he judged, Ruari's height at least. He wore a wetsuit that clung to a powerful chest and shoulders, and there was something lying on the sand next to him, attached to his waist with a chord. *A floatation device*, Ruari realised. The victim was a wild swimmer. His face had been covered up with a white cloth, and Ruari wondered if Alison had okayed that or if some well meaning bystander had inadvertently contaminated crucial evidence.

The victim lay flat on his back, his arms and legs flung out to the side. Something flickered in Ruari's brain and he climbed onto the wee stone wall next to the beach to get a better look. As he straightened up, he glimpsed something out of the corner of his eye, but didn't have time to register it before his gaze rested on the victim and horror seeped into his guts.

'Get down from there, you wee sicko,' hissed the PC guarding the perimeter, but Ruari barely heard him. The victim's arms lay out at his sides, his hands level with his waist. His legs were splayed at the hip, his feet apart, each pointing out to the side. 'Did you hear me?' the PC demanded. 'Get down or I'll do you for anti-social behaviour. What's the matter with you?'

Ruari was only vaguely conscious of Hannah's voice as she argued with the policeman, tried to explain that Ruari wasn't just a rubbernecker, that he would absolutely get down but please to just give him a second. The blood was pounding in his ears. Ruari blinked, hoping desperately to pull the scene into focus in a way that made sense. Then the crime scene tent went up and he couldn't see anything any more.

DAYLIGHT WAS JUST STARTING to fade, and powerful lights had been set up around the perimeter of the crime scene, as Cara leaned against the wall at the edge of the wee beach and took in the hive of activity. Lauren hovered nearby, writing a log of the comings and goings for the case file. Kevin was talking to a distressed young woman at the other end of the beach. Alison and her team were inside the tent, completing their preliminary examination of the body and the immediately surrounding area.

Alison was just a few years older than Cara, and had still been a lowly Scene of Crime Officer when Cara joined the force. They first met at a crime scene Cara had called in, when she was undercover as a Polish teenager gathering intel on a trafficking ring. After staging a panic attack the first time a 'client' was brought to her, Cara expertly manipulated the boss's twisted knight-in-shining-armour complex and had managed to finagle her way into 'working' his personal assistant. She typed and filed and listened wide-eyed to his tales of how his family had run the East End with a razor fist since the year dot, all the while fully aware that if he ever suspected she was police he would slit her throat without a second thought.

One morning she had arrived at his 'office' — a disused factory with a cheerful view of Riddrie Park Cemetery out one end and Barlinnie Prison out the other — to find a man sitting in the visitor's chair in front of her boss's desk, facing the window. Cara had established a routine of arriving at the crack of dawn -- *'she's a good one that lassie, not afraid of hard graft'* — the boss announced to a couple of his lackeys a few days earlier as Cara showed off the new accounts system she had devised while in fact taking copies of his supplier and customer lists.

So she was surprised, that morning, to find someone had beaten her. Irritated that she wouldn't have her customary couple of hours alone to snoop to her heart's content, she approached the man and offered him a cup of tea. He ignored her, so she tapped him on the shoulder and his head fell off.

She screamed and the boss and his lackeys stepped out from the shadows, beside themselves with laughter at their brilliant joke.

'Ye unnerstaun' ah've goat no choice when ah dae things like this?' he asked a few minutes later. One of the lackeys humphed the body into a coal-carry, splattering blood from the severed neck across the floor, while the other lackey brought up the rear with the head. They headed out the the reservoir, the one holding the head asking the other to dare him to try to play keepie-uppies with it.

The boss fixed Cara with such an intense stare she felt lightheaded. *'Ah dinnae relish it, but it's the joab. Ye unnerstaun' that, don't you, lass? Ah dinnae want ye tae think bad o' me.'* He reached over and squeezed her knee, and the sheepish smile he gave her haunted her for years. Frozen to the spot, Cara had forced herself to breathe steadily as she met his gaze and nodded. Then her lips twitched into a manic smile and she grinned and quipped it was nothing to lose the head over. He guffawed and told her to get the kettle on.

Cara had walked steadily to the outer office and radioed for backup. Alison was part of the team that arrived to process the two parts of the body the lackeys dropped in their attempt to scarper when they heard sirens approaching. The dead man turned out to be the brother of a girl who had told her family she was off to study in Scotland then disappeared.

Cara was perched at the back of a police van, trembling, trying unsuccessfully to hold it together, when Alison brought her over a cup of tea. She crouched in front of her and Cara braced herself for a round of sympathy that would finish her off. Alison pulled out her notebook and asked which direction the head had fallen in. They'd had each other's backs ever since.

'Scott Myers drowned,' Alison announced now with a deep yawn, yanking off her gloves as she joined Cara on the wall. 'I can tell you that much already. He was dead before any of the mutilation took place. Wisnae torture. I'd like to nut the halfwit that put that towel on his face, but given how public the site is, I can understand them not wanting kids to see the state of him.'

'Same as Bobby O'Brien?'

'Yep. Professional incisions around the neck, skin probably taken off in a oner.'

'Christ,' Cara muttered, as her stomach twisted. 'Face mutilation normally suggests personal, but this isn't feeling personal any more. Not in that way, at least.'

'There's bruising round his ankle that suggests someone swam up beneath him and yanked him under,' added Alison.

'What, like a scuba diver?'

Alison nodded. The loch lapped gently against the beach, its waters calm and glassy as the sun slipped below the horizon. 'If they managed to hold a trained swimmer underwater long enough to drown him, they would have to have some kind of breathing apparatus. It would have taken several minutes, at least.'

'Get onto every diving club or equipment rental place in Scotland,' Cara murmured. Lauren made a note.

'If the killer was kitted out with scuba gear, depending on what size his oxygen tank was, he could have swam to Ross Priory or even Luss.' Lauren said. 'I did a diving certification in Bali a few years ago. If he was only a few metres down, he could have stayed under for a good hour, even a bit more. He could have got pretty far in that time.'

'That's a long way to swim, though.'

Lauren shrugged. 'Swimming under the surface doesn't take it out of you as much as on the surface. You just kick yourself along, and if the current is behind you, you can even kind of let yourself be washed along.'

'Assuming the two cases are linked,' said Cara thoughtfully, 'and I think the identical face removals confirm that — then this killer is targeting men.'

'Especially given the paddleboarder,' Lauren added.

'The what?' asked Alison.

'A couple walking their dog on the beach spotted them talking as he headed out about nine this morning. It looked like he was helping her find something she dropped in the water, they said, They gave a description, but unless she comes forward I wouldn't hold out much hope of finding her.'

'Aye, but what's paddleboarding?'

'You stand up on a board, like a surfboard but a bit bigger, and paddle along like a gondola,' said Lauren. 'I've done it once, it's fun.'

Alison shook her head. 'What will they think of next?'

'Point is though, there was a woman alone in the area that the killer ignored.'

'That is interesting,' Cara nodded.

'He's targeting fit, good looking men,' said Kevin.

'He's targeting nice men,' said Lauren.

'Nice?'

'That woman Bobby O'Brien was dating, Natalie, she stressed over and over what a completely lovely person he was, and so did everyone else we talked to who knew him. Now this Scott Myers apparently helped out a strange woman this morning.'

'And that got him murdered?' said a voice. 'What's wrong with the world today?'

Cara turned and frowned as a figure stepped gingerly over the wet sand towards them. 'Liam. What are you doing here?'

'Evening folks,' Liam said with a brief salute as he crossed the sand. 'I was just passing and thought I'd pop in to see how my best team are getting on.'

'When's the last time you stepped foot on an active crime scene?' Alison asked dryly. 'And speaking of which, get those shoe covers on before I've no choice but to have you shot.'

Liam held up his hands in surrender. 'I won't deny it's been a while, ladies, but that's going to change. I don't think that pencil-pushing at the top is healthy. I believe that every serving officer shouldn't forget what it's like to get his — or hers — hands dirty. Do you not think, Cara?'

'If your dirty hands contaminate my crime scene —' Alison growled.

'I know, I know, you'll have me shot, I'll keep out your way, I promise.'

JADE'S TINY FLAT, bought with a deposit that had been the entirety of her parents' estate and mortgaged at a level that involved holding her breath and crossing her fingers on the first of every month, was her pride and joy. She'd not done much with it in the years Andy lived with her, ever conscious of the need to downplay the fact it was her flat and not theirs. That had been the deal when he moved in.

Looking back now, Jade couldn't even remember what made her so intransigent on that point, but she wouldn't budge. He paid his fair share of bills, but the mortgage was hers. When he packed his bags that final day, he had barely more than a suitcase to show for two years.

A few days after the attack, Jade had woken up and realised that the flat, with its flowery wallpaper and formica kitchen units, looked almost exactly as it had the day she moved in. It occurred to her that she'd been living in limbo, unable to make the flat hers because that would shine too harsh a light on the fact that it wasn't theirs. She'd got up that morning and started stripping wallpaper in her pyjamas.

Jade padded into the kitchen, pulled out a heavy iron pan, set onions to sauté in garlic oil as she assembled the spices needed for her favourite, intricate Moroccan tagine. It wasn't until the sweet potatoes and chickpeas were burbling away in a spicy tomato sauce that she noticed the jumper lying on the floor. *Andy*, she thought, an unbearable lump forming in her throat as she held it to her and breathed the scent of him in.

He had chucked her, she thought, misery washing over her. They'd started fighting about something stupid and he'd said it was over and he had left. She sank to the floor and gathered the jumper to her, unable to believe he had really gone.

Her head thudded where she had hit it on the stone wall in the Campsies when she escaped the night before, the dried blood around her black eye made her face feel tight. She needed to tell Andy what had happened. It wasn't fair to let him find out on the grapevine. He'd left the address for her, somewhere, so she could forward on post. She had to get to him. She had to tell him before someone else did.

She scrabbled to her feet, holding the jumper tightly, staring wildly around the wee flat. The note with the address was here somewhere, it had to be. Or maybe she could phone him? Maybe he would come round -- that would be better than them trying to have a serious talk with whichever of his footie pals he was crashing with.

No, she thought in frustration, Hannah had forced her to delete his number from her phone the day before. *I'll give it to you if you really need it, but we need to get temptation off your phone. It's for your own good. We've all been there.*

The smell of spicy tomato sauce hit Jade's nostrils and she stared at the steaming tagine in confusion. What was she doing cooking in the middle of all this? She needed to find Andy — the police — the police were waiting for her. She had to give a statement, had to try to remember what happened — her head pounded, she couldn't think straight — the nurse said she'd have a wee a headache the next day. The police had tried to take a statement from her at the hospital, she thought in panic, but she couldn't remember anything.

She was so confused. She just wanted it all to go away. She just wanted Andy.

Jade touched her face, but it wasn't swollen.

The black eye wasn't there. Her cheekbone and temple felt normal, there was no cut on her forehead, no plaster, no stitches. That couldn't be right, it didn't make sense. Her face was healed.

It had all happened a long time ago. That's why she was cooking. That's why her face was fine.

Andy had a baby.

Jade backed away from the cooker, slid to the floor against the fridge, holding the jumper to her.

She closed her eyes, took some deep breaths. Forced herself to count slowly to ten. Then backwards. Then in French, though she was fairly sure she'd made at least three of the numbers up and possibly said one in German. It had been nothing but a wee episode, she thought, as pins and needles ripped through her and her heart fluttered in her chest.

A wave of sadness washed over her as she thought of Bobby rubbing her back with his big hands the other day. *That you back with us?* he had said. *Aye Bobby,* she thought sadly. *That's me back.* It had just been a wee one, she thought with relief. She had remembered, she had brought herself back before going charging out the flat round to make a nuisance of herself when the baby probably needed its dinner or something.

Actually making it to Andy's once a week was more than enough, she thought with a shudder. She smiled as she remembered once giggling with Hannah that she was the literal worst-case scenario ex. Plenty of people worried about an ex hanging about the fringes of their relationship, but few had to put up with one actually rocking up and banging on the front door on a regular basis.

'Ach serves him right,' Hannah had cackled, knocking back her third gin and tonic

Amy had warned her that things might get worse before they got better, Jade reminded herself. 'Your mind is desperately trying to protect you from something, and it's not going to give up without a fight,' she said.

Jade's phone buzzed and she jumped a mile. It was a text from Hannah about the American reality show they were both obsessed with, but when she unlocked the screen, a Facebook memory filled the screen.

It was of her and Andy posing at a friend's wedding four years ago. Him in his kilt and dickie bow, her in a dress she'd got for a song at one of those pop up shops that normally sell tat, but somehow magically produced a gorgeous floaty number that Jade was fairly confident made her look like some wood nymph or fairy. 'It was seven quid!' she'd crowed gleefully whenever she was complimented on it that day.

A funny, tight feeling formed in her tummy as she stared at the photo. She was wearing too much makeup, she noticed in surprise. That wasn't her style at all. She must have seen some glam makeup look on Youtube or something and decided to try it, she thought, rolling her eyes at her past self. What a fanny.

She started to reply to Hannah's text, but her fingers were still clumsy and clammy. She put the phone down in irritation and went to stir the tagine. As she reached for the wooden spoon, she stood on the jumper and her heart leapt into her mouth again.

'Oh for fuck's sake,' she muttered aloud, kicking it out the way — then she stopped. That *was* Andy's jumper.

Her gran had knitted it for him the first Christmas they were together. It was a dark grey, wiry, scratchy monstrosity with a neck hole that was too wee for his head to get through without shoving for several minutes and nearly ripping his ears off. Every time Gran came round for months after that Christmas, she would pointedly ask why he wasn't wearing it, and Andy would slink into the bedroom, emerging minutes later red-faced and sweating and mortified, wearing the jumper that would be ideal for scouring an oven.

Gran would smile sweetly and say how happy she was that he loved it. When Jade finally clicked she was doing it on purpose, she berated herself for going soft. She had lived with her Gran for well over twenty years, she should have known right away.

Andy would never have taken it with him when he left, Jade thought now, staring at the offending pile of sheep's bum wool on the floor. That's why she kept coming across it. But what the hell had it been doing on her kitchen floor? Or her bedroom floor a few days ago, for that matter. She remembered now, a week or so after the breakup, Hannah ordering her to throw it out. Jade protested that was too harsh, and they'd compromised on shoving it at the back of the airing cupboard.

Jade reached for her phone and pulled up the contact she had saved the day before.

'Can I come and see you tomorrow morning?' she asked when Amy answered. 'I think I want to do that hypnosis.'

ARE YOU DOING THIS? Cara thought. Alec McAvoy lay preternaturally still on the hotel bed, hooked up to what appeared to be dozens of machines, beeping and whirring and exhaling. The room was small, made claustrophobic with all the equipment, and a police guard had been stationed outside the door twenty-four hours a day for two years.

It could have been a coincidence that Bobby O'Brien was found in something that resembled first position, but not Scott Myers too. Whoever this killer was, he knew how Alec ordered his special victims to be displayed -- but McAvoy had been unconscious for two years.

'He's far from brain dead,' the consultant, a tall black woman with closely cropped hair, a faint French accent and a no nonsense manner had said. 'He responds to pain stimuli, his eyes react to light, he has even attempted to breathe when we remove him from the ventilator for a short time. He simply refuses to wake. Really, he is simply in an extremely deep sleep.'

'Is he aware of his surroundings? Can he hear us?' Cara asked.

The consultant shrugged. 'That is the age-old question. Many patients who have awoken from similar comas have been able to recall things that were said to them when they were unconscious, others might have heard at the time but can't remember. Others still, describe it as a black fog of nothing. And of course for those who never wake, we have no idea. So your guess is as good as mine.'

'Do you know who he is?'

The consultant nodded. 'He is my patient. That is all I allow myself to know. If he is aware of his surroundings, I suspect he does not appreciate the nurses' taste in television, but of course I don't know anything about that.' She smiled and left Cara alone with Alec and the machines.

There was no way he could be communicating with someone, she told herself. She wasn't sure who she was trying to convince. Could he have set it up before? It was almost precisely two years later, was the timing relevant? Had he primed a puppet to come to life every two years — forevermore?

Cara held onto the bars at the side of the bed, fighting against an impulse to scream and shake him. To unplug the machines and run away. She'd read somewhere that it wasn't as easy to pull the plug as TV dramas made out. That it wasn't like unplugging a lamp or TV, that there were locks and codes and back-up generators in place. Even so, they were alone. He was unconscious, entirely vulnerable. She could kill him if she was really determined.

After a moment, Cara let go of the bars and buzzed for the young PC guarding the door to let her out. She wouldn't kill Alec McAvoy in his hospital bed. She wouldn't give him the satisfaction.

She wanted him fully conscious and aware, led hand-cuffed into the very same courtroom he once held rapt as a crown advocate. To sit in impotent silence in the defendant's box as his crimes were debated without his input, to read lurid headlines about the celebrity lawyer turned psycho, and hear the jeers of the sort of vigilante mobs who liked to hang about outside the courthouse for a good old shout. She wanted him to be sentenced, to hear the slam of a prison door rattling in his ears, to be cornered and trapped and controlled, marched through endless days of carefully monitored monotony.

Samira was right, Cara thought as she waited for the lift. What drove Alec McAvoy was power. Somehow, some day, she would ensure he lost every scrap of his, and she would be certain that he was aware of every second of it.

6

D amn it wasn't even Memorial Day yet and already it was hotter than hades. Cody Capouski swung her 1976 Mustang Cobra into the parking lot and made up her mind, as she did every single summer, that this was the year she'd finally sacrifice style for a car with actual working air con. Even with every window down and the fan allegedly blowing cold air on her, Cody felt like she needed three showers before she could pass as an actual human again.

She killed the engine, took a swig of lukewarm Gatorade from the passenger seat, and drummed her fingers on the steering wheel as she considered her plan. The prison was squat and ugly, a bunch of grey buildings and a grey yard surrounded by a few scrubby patches of parched grass and bordered with high barbed wire fencing. Somehow it was dull and creepy in equal measures, though the buzzard ominously circling above the yard definitely gave it a little Stephen King flavour.

She leaned back in the seat, feeling sweat trickle down the back of her neck. Nobody was going to be like, *oh yeah you got us, we totally lost a death row prisoner and kept it quiet for two years,* no matter how she approached it. Except they had, and she was going to blow it open, somehow.

Ever since that day, just over two years ago, when she had been turned away after showing up for the interview she had lined up and confirmed with Stuart Henderson, she had known something was up. The Scottish dude had been singing like a canary about his every crime to anyone who wanted to listen — and a whole bunch of people who'd really have preferred not to listen — since the moment he was sentenced. And now all of a sudden he lost his voice?

At first, Cody figured his legal team had him on lockdown. There had been talk that his claim that his wife controlling him was laying groundwork for an appeal. If they were going to go for insanity and at least get his death sentence commuted, it made sense they needed to shut him up for a while. Stuart Henderson was a lot of things, Cody thought, but he was not nuts. Then months went by, and no appeal.

Eventually Cody got an interview with one of the partners at the firm under the pretence that it was for a piece about false convictions on death row. Four percent of all prisoners on death row were innocent, she had read, and pitched a piece on the appeals system to one of the only magazine contacts she had left that still had a freelance budget. She managed to get the lawyer round to the subject of Henderson easily enough, and asked him about the appeal rumours. He laughed, shook his head and stated categorically that he believed everybody deserved a fair trial and the best defence possible in a free country — but all the same, Stuart Henderson was guilty as sin and he hoped he fried. There would be no further appeals to his conviction.

So then Cody started talking to prison staff. She also slept with a couple of the prison staff, though in the case of the guard with the thighs she'd happily start a whole church just to worship, that was no hardship. She figured out their hangouts, casually joined the crew a few times, and gradually, gently started to bring the subject of Henderson up.

Everybody shut down. Literally, in the case of the guy with the thighs, which was a double disappointment. Like, blank walls. Nobody knew anything about Stuart Henderson, and they wouldn't say if they did.

Cody was not a woman to give up easily. She wanted to know what the hell had happened to Stuart Henderson, and she wasn't going to stop until she did. For a long time it seemed like she was staring at the unusual and unwelcome prospect of total failure.

Until now. She still had to play it right, but finally, she had come across a thing that might just be something.

After hitting eight billion blank walls with every avenue she could think of, one of her casual chats with one of the prison staff paid off. Death row, it turned out, got special catering. *Not, like, fancy food or anything*, the guy rushed to assure her. *It's the same old gross glop we feed the rest of 'em, but it gets ordered in from outside.*

Apparently there was an issue a few years back when there was a peadophile on the row and some kitchen staff set out to save the State a job and poison him. *Stupid really, on account of he wasn't gonna leave us alive one way or another, but seems it woulda opened us up to a whole world of shit with lawsuits and stuff.* So they started ordering in meals from some outside catering company who had no idea who they were feeding.

According to official records, death row currently housed nine men, including Henderson. Cody tracked down the catering company and got hold of a copy of the prison's weekly orders for the past year.

Eight meals.

Either Henderson was on a pretty serious hunger strike, or they were no longer feeding him for other reasons.

Like that he wasn't there.

Cody got out of the car and wiped the sweat from the back of her neck and forehead with the sleeve of an old sweater she found in the back seat. She spritzed her face with some stupid spray that promised to give her a cool and youthful glow though she was pretty sure it was just $14 water in a can, and started to cross the parking lot.

A second buzzard had joined the first, and they were swooping in lazy circles above the condemned men. Through four sets of barbed wire fences she could see a bunch of guys in jumpsuits wandering around. A couple were lifting weights, though most sat still and listless.

'Hey I have an appointment with the governor,' Cody said to the receptionist. The full blast of air con hit her the second she opened the door and she kind of wished she could stand still for a second with her eyes closed and just soak in the cool.

'Sure honey, what's your name?' the receptionist was new. *Retired cop*, thought Cody, taking in the woman's salt and pepper hair and cynical smile.

'Oh you're the reporter for the profile piece?' she said as Cody signed in. 'He's waiting for you. He's been trying on different ties all morning, trying to decide what makes him most look devoted to truth and justice and the American way.'

'Awesome,' said Cody, as she stepped through the metal detector.

'WHY AM I ANGRY WITH HIM?' Jade repeated. Amy sat in an

armchair that dwarfed her tiny frame, holding her ever present notebook and pen. Jade stood by the tiny attic window, watching ant-like folk cut about George Square in the rain.

'Well primarily because he tried to kill me.' Jade leaned her forehead against the window, grateful for the coolness of the glass, sighed. 'Then there's the fact that he failed.'

'You're angry that he failed to murder you?'

'Well no, obviously, but —' Jade turned, leaned against the windowsill, crossed her arms, tried to figure out a way of explaining what she meant. 'Okay, I've got this one client who, whatever I say for him to do, he responds 'I'll try.' Honest to god I could nut him, it drives me mad. I don't even know why. I come over all Yoda. *Do or do not.* And this, it's like — you're a serial killer, you've got one job.'

'It's interesting how you always refer to him as a serial killer,' commented Amy.

'Well what would you call him? Buddy old pal? Me old china? Late for dinner?'

'A serial killer is someone who commits three or more murders over a period of at least a month, usually with a significant cooling-off period in between.'

'Well I don't mean like — I'm not being official. I just mean the way you'd call Hannibal Lecter a serial killer.'

'Hannibal Lecter meets the definition.'

'You know what I mean.'

'I want to know what you mean. So far, you've consistently referred to the man who attacked you as a serial killer, when, according to the police, there is nothing to suggest that he so much as attacked anyone other than you.'

'Well — it's what he does, isn't it? It's what they do. I saw they found another body yesterday. I just saw the headline when I walked past a newsagents, I'm trying not to think about it too much, but it said second body, so it must be related to Bobby somehow.

'So they don't stop at one, do they? What are the chances my attacker was just some normal wee guy who wouldn't hurt a fly, just going about his business until he clapped eyes on me and took the ultimate maddy?' Jade hesitated, a coldness creeping down her spine. 'Do you think that's it? Do you think I set him off?'

'Absolutely not,' said Amy firmly. 'I'm just curious as to why your mind is so certain on this point. I'm wondering if you know something about him you're not consciously aware of yet.'

'I -- see.' Jade shook her head, feeling icy chills cascade over her. 'No.' Amy's expression was impassive. Jade shook her head again. 'Definitely not. I don't know anything. I don't remember anything. That's the whole point.'

'Okay. That's fine.'

'He attacked me twice,' Jade blurted. Her stomach had taken on a heavy, hollow feeling. She shifted her weight, the windowsill digging into her bum. She wished she were sitting the comfy sofa where she could curl up. She rubbed her arms, though it wasn't cold, wrapped her cardigan more tightly around her.

'I don't mean literally. I mean — he tried to strangle me, but more than that —' She sighed helplessly, feeling the tell-tale fluttering of her heart, pins and needles dancing on the tips of her fingers. She forced herself to take a deep, slow, breath. 'He took away my — I don't even know what to call it. My certainty. The episodes where I forget it's now aren't the worst bits.

'It's the never quite trusting myself. Never knowing whether or not what I think or feel at any given moment is real. The other day, I was at work and someone dropped a barbell on the hard part of the floor. This almighty bang resounded around the gym and everyone jumped a mile, but I just froze. I didn't know whether or not I'd got a fright. There's times I worry I'd just sit there if a building was on fire or something because I spend so much time talking myself out of being scared, convincing myself it's not real, that I've forgotten that sometimes it is real.

'Like the boy that cried wolf, but inside my own head. I hate him for that more than I hate him for trying to strangle me.'

'Is that why you want to try the hypnosis?' Amy asked, her voice gentle. 'You were quite set against it before.'

'Want is a strong word,' Jade replied dryly, 'but I'll try anything. I've had enough.'

'OH PRAISE SWEET MERCIFUL JESUS —'

Jesse Coleman, soaking wet from the hike through rivers and streams, fell to his knees and kissed the dry mulch of long fallen leaves.

The woman looked anxiously at her two partners, not wanting to alarm Jesse, but wanting to know why it took so much longer than it was supposed to. Dawn would be breaking within the hour. Neither of her partners would meet her eye.

She crouched next Jesse, put her hand on his shoulder. He flinched, an automatic reflex, and she drew back.

'I'm sorry ma'am. I didn't mean to startle you.'

'No problem.' She forced a smile, made her voice as light as she could. 'But we need to get moving. Morning ain't far off.'

'Of course, ma'am, whatever you say. I just never thought

I'd touch real dirt again. The earth is fuckin' glorious, man. Praise Him.'

'You bet. Let's go.'

Jesse scrambled to his feet. The woman gave him a reassuring smile, beckoned for him to follow her through the path she had marked out through the thick Tennessee forest. The two guys brought up the rear, destroying markers and footprints as they went.

By the time they reached the edge of the nature reserve and their vehicle, the first pink shards of dawn could be seen streaking through the night sky. It would be light soon, she thought. Shit. In the distance, the droning wail of the prison alarm suddenly filled the air. The woman's heart fell. Too quick. If all had gone to plan, they wouldn't have noticed his absence for hours.

Jesse waited silently for instructions, fear and acceptance playing in his brown eyes as the alarm droned and searchlights criss crossed the light blue sky. 'Didn't never think I'd get this far,' he said softly.

'It ain't done yet,' snapped the taller man, in a tone that invited no contradiction. Safe in the shadows, the woman rolled her eyes. He always took charge the moment they were far enough away to start to feel safe. 'We go get us some breakfast in Nashville, hiding in plain sight, exactly like we planned.'

He rolled open the door of the soccer mom people carrier that never got pulled over, and they all clambered in. The new guy drove, as agreed. The taller guy slumped in the passenger seat, but the woman could sense tension emanating from him. She noticed Jesse looking curiously at the baby seat.

'I toss cracker crumbs all around it,' she grinned,

affecting a cheer she didn't feel. 'For realism's sake, you know?'

'You ain't just a pretty face.'

'No, sir.' She wiggled one eyebrow, a trick that took her several weeks of dedicated practice in college to perfect. She leaned over and snuggled into Jesse's side, a young woman dosing against her boyfriend's shoulder as their friends drove them home from a party. Jesse followed her lead and leaned back against the seat, affected sleep.

The new guy put the van into drive and pull out of the parking lot, careful to stick exactly to the speed limit even as the prison alarm thudded in their ears. The woman opened one eye, watched the searchlights streaking through the woods. They hadn't even reached the spot where the minivan had been parked yet. She felt Jesse tense and gave him a brief, reassuring smile. The lights of the approaching city twinkled in the distance.

It was going to be fine, the woman thought as they pulled onto the freeway without getting stopped. She was crazy to worry. They had done the job right, just like they always did.

'I SOLEMNLY, sincerely and truly declare that I will tell the truth, the whole truth and nothing but the truth.'

The bailiff nodded and Amy took her seat in the witness box. The courtroom was silent; Amy could feel all eyes on her as she forced herself to sit up straight and face the crown advocate, who shuffled through her notes before approaching Amy with a brief, polite smile that didn't reach her eyes. Though the High Court in Glasgow couldn't be much more different from the Dallas County criminal court, a tiny part of her always half expected to see Stuart sitting in the defendant's box, blinking at her from behind his steel-rimmed glasses.

'How long has the defendant been your patient?'

'Just over a year,' said Amy clearly. The crown advocate had introduced herself in a clipped girls' school accent as Miss Hamilton. Her face was impassive, but Amy detected a trace of nerves in her cool, blue eyes. She was young, with a freckled nose and dark blonde hair escaping from beneath her barrister's wig.

'Can you explain for the court why you believe that the defendant was acting in self defence when she killed her husband?' she asked.

Amy nodded and took a breath, her first words running through her mind. It was crucial that she got this right. Not only was her client Shona depending on her, so were her four kids. If Shona went down for murder, they were going into the system. The eldest was just six and Shona's mother was bedridden with gout. Shona's sister had been in the frame to foster her nieces and nephews until the night before the trial opened, when she fell off the wagon and tried to steal a bus full of people waiting to leave Buchanan Bus Station.

'They'll never let her take them now,' Shona had whispered when Amy visited her in the remand cell. 'If they go to strangers, that's it, I'll never see them again.' Her voice was high and tight with shock, her eyes unnaturally wide. She clutched Amy's hand as though without it she might drown.

'Shona Kennedy killed her husband because she feared for her own life, and for her children's lives,' Amy said now and out of the corner of her eye she thought she caught one of the jurors give an almost imperceptible nod.

All morning, as the prosecution outlined the forensic

evidence detailing how Shona had caused the severe cerebral bleed which killed her husband almost instantly with her Auntie's antique brass candlesticks, Amy had kept her eyes locked on Shona as though she could transport a physical beam of support across the courtroom. Shona had been silent, watching the proceedings with wide-eyed terror, only once emitting a moan when the candlesticks were admitted into evidence and her Auntie stood up to shout that she was glad they had ridded the world of such an evil wee shite.

'Evidence has already shown that James Kennedy was fast asleep in front of the television at the time of the attack. Perhaps you could explain just what sort of threat was posed to the defendant from a man who was snoring?'

There was a muted titter, that someone swiftly tried to turn into a cough. Amy thought it came from the press gallery, and swallowed an impulse to snap at Miss Hamilton to show some respect.

'Shona Kennedy had suffered mental, emotional and physical abuse from her husband throughout their eight year marriage,' Amy said, addressing Miss Hamilton, but conscious of the jury's eyes on her. 'The effects of such a sustained period of intimate partner violence are significant and well documented. Specifically, the victim reaches a state of chronic fear, which means that she fears for her life on a more or less constant basis.'

'Be that as it may, the fact remains that James Kennedy was unconscious and as such, the defendant was in no actual danger at the time of the attack.'

'Is that a question?'

The lawyer's face fell for an instant and her cheeks flushed, then she swiftly recovered with a cool smile. She's going to be good, Amy thought. She was being careful to specify *at the time of the attack* over and over. There was no question that Shona had been in immediate, physical danger from her husband at many, many other times.

'Why do you say that the defendant feared for her life at the time of the attack?' Miss Hamilton asked.

Amy turned to the jury. 'Scientists are able to see the journey of fear through the brain. Think of it like a smoke alarm. When something happens to cause fear, the brain sets off a warning signal that sets off a series of signals that activate fight or flight mode. This is a very specific process with clear physical symptoms, that shows up clearly in brain scans. Most likely everyone in this courtroom has experienced it at some point or other — the tightening of the stomach, heart thumping, pins and needles. It's primal, caveman stuff — our reptilian brain taking over.

'What we are just beginning to understand is the way in which those series of signals can cause permanent damage in the brain. You've heard of things like Post Traumatic Stress Disorder? That's when a trauma has been so great, fear so extreme that it actually alters the structure of the brain, sometimes permanently. It can affect the brain's ability to tell the difference between present danger and the memory of danger — scans have shown that a flashback can create as much, or even more, terror as the original trauma.

'A constant state of fear has a similar effect. The brain gets in the habit of constantly flashing *danger — warning — alert* that after a while it doesn't need to be triggered by something happening, it just sets itself off, out of habit if you like. Over years and years of abuse, Shona's brain had learned to be in a constant state of terror from her husband.'

'But still there was no actual danger at the time of the attack,' snapped Miss Hamilton. She turned to address the jury. 'Under Scottish law, there must be imminent danger to the life of the defendant for a verdict of self defence to be returned. Whatever Shona Kennedy's brain may have been *flashing* —'

She held up her hands in air quotes with an expression of mocking disbelief, but Amy saw two of the jurors' mouths tighten and one frowned. She'd overplayed her hand, Amy thought. She was losing the jury. A flicker of hope flared to life.

' — at the time of the attack, the defendant Shona Kennedy was in no *actual* — '

'— Or reasonable belief they are going to be attacked,' Amy cut her off. 'I am not a lawyer, but I believe that the reasonable expectation of an attack also forms part of the definition of self defence.'

'The victim was asleep,' Miss Hamilton fired back. 'It is hardly reasonable to expect attack from an unconscious man, therefore —'

'Three weeks before his death, James Kennedy was apparently asleep in front of the TV,' Amy said, speaking quickly. 'The sun had come out that afternoon and Shona could see a thin layer of dust on the windowsill behind the sofa. She knew her husband would punish her if he woke up and noticed it. Not because of malfunctioning brain patterns, but because he had done exactly that on several prior occasions.

'As she leaned over him, as carefully as she could, to clean the windowsill behind him, he suddenly grabbed her by the collar of her T shirt and held her immobile while he head butted her and broke her nose. You can still see her bruises right now.'

Amy gestured towards the defendant's box and was gratified to note several juror's looking over at Shona's ravaged face. 'Shona Kennedy attacked her husband and caused his death because she feared for her life at all times.'

'Thank you, no further questions at this time.'

As Amy left the courthouse a few minutes later, she was satisfied she had done her best for her client. Her mind was already drifting back to this morning's hypnosis session. She had promised Jade that she would discuss everything she had said under hypnosis at the next session. She had sensed that trying to talk her through it too soon would prove over-whelming, but now she remembered how quiet Jade was when she left the office. She would give her a quick phone just to check in as soon as she got home, Amy resolved, feeling in her coat pocket for her bike's keys.

'Y'alright there missus?' The young man, little more than a boy, in an ill fitting suit, nearly crashed into Amy when she stopped short just before she reached her bike.

'Sorry,' she muttered, forcing a smile. 'Could you do me a massive favour? Could you look into my bike basket there and tell me what's in it? I — I can see something, and, I've got a bit of a phobia about mice.I'm scared it's —'

'Aye, no bother,' the wee guy said, 'you're okay though. No mice here. It's just a pair of socks.'

'THE CAR PARK at the foot of Conic Hill probably has CCTV, and check with the pub as well. Lauren can you get on to that? Have you got anywhere with scuba diving clubs?' Cara paced her office, sharpie pen in hand. The whiteboards were back.

'Only thing I have so far is that some gear was rented in Greenock on Saturday morning for the weekend and not yet returned. Name was C. MacGregor, they're trying to hunt down the ID and details, but they had a flood yesterday so it's all a bit chaotic.'

'Okay, keep an eye on that. He might well have his own

equipment of course, but he must have trained, got some kind of certification, maybe? He could have done it abroad, but is there some kind of governing body in Scotland?'

'I think there is, I'll look into it,' Lauren muttered, scribbling in her notebook.

'Okay, what do we know about Scott Myers? Kevin?'

Cara pulled a fresh whiteboard nearer, took the top off a new pen.

Kevin cleared his throat. 'He grew up in Canada, just outside Vancouver, though his mum came from Glasgow and the family visited every couple of years. He moved over here with a Scottish girl about four years ago, and decided to stay on even when they finished. He stayed in Maryhill, worked in finance, travelled to Edinburgh and London a lot, seems to have been a fitness fanatic —'

'Like Bobby O'Brien?' interjected Cara.

'Aye, but more into the outdoorsy stuff than pumping iron. Last summer he scaled some fancy cliff up Glencoe way, I think. It's meant to be the go-to challenge for rock climbers, and he's done the Matterhorn in Switzerland, whatever that is.'

'That's the mountain on muesli boxes,' said Lauren.

'That right?'

She nodded.

'But still, extreme fitness, single after a long term relationship,' Cara muttered, scribbling a dizzying mind map on the board.

'Lately, his thing has been wild swimming,' continued Kevin. 'He was training to do some famous island to island race in Scandinavia somewhere, that's what he was doing out on his own so early yesterday. Great guy, pal to everyone, absolutely no one who would so much as spit in his cornflakes.'

'Sounds familiar. Any solid connection to Bobby as yet?'

Kevin and Lauren both shook their heads, and Cara leaned against her desk, tapped her pen against her teeth, looking over her scribbles. 'What about to Jade McFadyen?'

'I thought of that,' said Kevin, 'but nothing I've come across so far. He trained at a different gym and no friends in common have popped up so far.'

'Where's Samira?' asked Cara suddenly. 'Did she speak to Jade about Bobby?'

'She got a phone call just as we came in here,' Kevin said. 'Said she'd join us when she could.'

'Okay. We're waiting for Alison's full report. I gather some possible trace DNA was found, despite the rain.'

Kevin nodded. 'Results should be in any minute. I know they've been pulling out the stops, Jack never came home last night till the middle of the night.'

'Then let's pause until we hear more from —'

Cara was cut off as Samira barged through the door, knocking even as she flung it open. 'I've just spoken to a family who were at the Balmaha car park yesterday morning,' she announced. 'They were camping last night so didn't hear anything about what happened until they got back this afternoon, but get this. They talked to a woman as they were unpacking their car that morning. She was a runner, just setting off to run up Conic. Flaming red hair and a wee skinny slip of a thing.'

'What time was this?' Cara demanded.

'Just before seven.'

'And the couple on the beach saw him with the paddle-boarder at the back of nine? It probably takes about two, three hours to go up and down Conic if you stick to a decent clip, right?' said Cara. Lauren nodded. 'We need to find this red haired woman.'

'No need,' said Samira. 'The family asked her to take a picture of them setting off on their trip, but something was wrong with their camera, so she took it on her phone and emailed it to them. The mum just forwarded the email to me with the woman's address. *Kerr2dance@hotmail.com*. It's Amy Kerr. Doctor, Amy Kerr. Mrs Amy Henderson. She was metres away when Scott Myers was murdered.'

'Who still has a hotmail address?' Kevin murmured as Cara felt a chill wash over her. The teenager who found Bobby O'Brien's body also mentioned a red haired woman who had disappeared by the time the police arrived.

'It's not a coincidence,' Samira stated, staring at Cara as though defying her to object. Cara had no intention of doing so.

'Of course it isn't.'

'Find out if Amy Kerr has a scuba diving license,' Samira ordered. Lauren glanced at Cara for confirmation.

'It's not a coincidence, but let's not get ahead of ourselves, we don't know what it is,' Cara said, but nodded at Lauren. 'All the same, it won't hurt to check.'

'We need to bring her in,' insisted Samira. 'Scare her into finally telling us everything she —'

'Cara?' Alison knocked softly as she poked her head around the door.

'It's like Central station all of a sudden,' Cara smiled and beckoned Alison in. 'Come and join the party.'

Her old friend looked ashen. Cara's smile faded and molten dread pooled in her stomach. 'Can I help you, Alison?' she said, more sharply than she intended.

'Could I have a word?'

Cara spotted Kevin's husband Jack hovering in the corridor behind Alison, and she sighed impatiently, feeling her heart start to pound. 'For heaven's sake come in properly both of you and spit it out,' she ordered, as she half wondered whether she would hit her desk or the floor if her knees gave way. 'If you've found something we all need to hear about it without delay.'

'I think you and I should speak alone first.' Alison spoke gently but firmly. 'Could everyone please give us the room for a moment?'

Cara was only barely aware of Samira, Kevin and Lauren filing silently from her office. For a mad moment she wanted to shout them back, insist on carrying on the meeting, anything so she wouldn't have to hear what Alison was about to tell her. Lauren shut the door softly behind them and Cara leaned over, clutched the desk, taking deep breaths to try to stop herself from fainting.

'Is he dead?' she asked.

'MIND if I put the radio on?' Roddy asked, as Jade glanced over her shoulder before switching lanes to overtake the lane of cars slowing to get on to the Erskine bridge. 'I feel like I might drop off, and it's too soon to subject you to my snoring.'

'No bother, go ahead,' Jade said. She remembered too late that the pre-set radio in her car was the cheesy pop station she loved. 'I have the taste in music of a thirteen year old girl and I'm not sorry,' she grinned, wishing she'd had the presence of mind to turn it to something slightly more credible.

It had been fine, Jade thought with a smile, as they reached Great Western Road and immediately hit traffic. She had Mondays free of clients or classes, so when she left Amy's office she had impulsively texted Roddy to see if he wanted to come kayaking with her. He replied almost immediately that he couldn't think of a better way to spend the afternoon. Before she could chicken out, she arranged to pick him up outside the café where they had met. She had insisted on being the one to drive, and appreciated that he hadn't argued.

Maybe this was it, Jade thought, and a wee sliver of happiness danced over her. It wasn't as though it was love at first sight with Roddy or anything like that, but that wasn't the point. She felt normal. She'd felt normal the whole afternoon, nothing but the standard prickle of first date nerves here and there. She was already composing the report she would text to Hannah as soon as she dropped him off. Maybe the hypnosis had done the trick already.

After a brief lesson at the rental place in Luss, Jade had picked up the basics fairly quickly, though she'd had to fish Roddy out Loch Lomond twice when he hit a wave at an awkward angle and tipped in. He'd had a good sense of humour about it, she'd noted, even though it took him several tries to clamber back in and his teeth were chattering when they got back to the beach. Conversation had dried up a bit on the drive home, but it was a comfortable enough silence.

'I've no patience for music snobs,' he said now. 'I once had a pal say to me that he didn't like any music anybody else had ever heard of, and all I could think was, is that no' another way of saying you like shite music? If it's any good, surely at least somebody else would like it too?'

'That's what I think,' laughed Jade. 'Who's got time for depressing shite with no tune?'

'I don't demand much of my music, but it needs to have a bloody tune,' Roddy said. 'And a recognisable chorus I can sing along to.'

'Agreed.'

'I went to a jazz bar in Chicago once, and I sat there thinking, how is nobody else noticing they've forgotten the tune?'

Jade laughed. 'Is that where you lived?'

'Sorry?'

'Didn't you say you'd lived in the States?'

'No — well aye, I did, but I was just visiting Chicago. California, was where I lived. San Francisco.'

'I've always wanted to go there. I read a book about Alcatraz when I was wee and got weirdly obsessed.'

'What's this lassie's name?' Roddy asked, gesturing towards the radio.

'She's American and she's got enormous hair,' Jade replied with a shrug. 'That's all I know about her. But, like, huge. The biggest hair you've ever seen in your whole life.'

'I like her already.'

The song blended seamlessly into the next one, a chart hit from the mid nineties.

'Now we're talking,' shouted Roddy. 'I touched a girl's bum for the first time to this one.'

But the car gave a violent jerk and Jade belatedly realised she had slammed the brakes on.

'What the — what are you doing? What happened —'

His voice sounded distant and distorted as blood roared in Jade's ears. 'I — sorry —' she muttered, waving at the car honking angrily behind. *Shit, shit, shit.* This wasn't supposed to be happening now. She managed to pull over, hitting the kerb with a thud, and fumbled for her seatbelt, gasping for breath. Roddy leaned over and yanked the handbrake on.

'What the — what's going on? Jade? Are you okay?'

Hot pins and needles stabbed at her as her throat closed up and vision tunnelled. *Don't faint*, a tiny part of her silently begged. *Don't end up in hospital again. Breathe. Just keep breathing.*

Images flew at her. Icy fingers closed around her ankle. A sweet, sickly smell filling her nostrils.

'Jade?' Roddy's voice was gentle now. He'd realised, she thought dully. Noticed she was a nutter.

She was waiting for her carry-out Indian the night Andy told her it was over.

'Noo,' she moaned softly, distantly aware of Roddy's hand closing over hers.

She'd been hiccupping and wracked with dry, empty sobs, barely able to see out eyes so red and raw. The wee guy who took her order had been clearly petrified. When he said they were out of her favourite aubergine fritters her eyes had filled up again and he'd nearly had a hairy canary. His mum came out, shoved him out the way and took Jade in her arms, murmuring into her hair that whoever he was, he wasn't worth it.

'I don't even remember what we started fighting about,' she'd hiccupped to the wee lady. 'It just came out of nowhere and then he was gone.'

Then she'd been walking home, swinging the hot bag with the tantalising smells. She'd nearly swung it off the edge of her finger at one point and tears had welled up again at the thought of her precious takeaway ending up in a puddle. She turned off Duke Street onto a wee side street and was nearly blinded by the full headlights that greeted her. She remembered gesturing to the driver to turn the beams down, first with her hand then with a choice finger. Then she was in the car and her Indian was in a puddle after all.

She remembered still feeling the tight ring the handle of the plastic bag had made on her finger as the car sped round Alexandra Park, up through Riddrie and Provanmill, past

Robroyston and into the suburbs Jade and her gran always derided impossibly posh.

'They're all bought houses in there,' *Gran sniffed once upon a time as the bus swung round the Torrance roundabout on their way to visit the Fintry Granny. She shook her head at the absurdity of shelling out hard-earned money for a house.* 'I'll bet you half of them cannae afford carpets.'

'Jade, do you need help?' said Roddy gently. She could feel him squeezing her hand. 'Do you — should I phone an ambulance?'

'No, no, no —' She shook her head frantically, tried to force her face into something resembling a reassuring smile.

'Okay,' he said. 'I'm here. Just — take your time.'

It had been a bright evening. She had been able see the outline of the Campsies silhouetted against the purple sky through the windscreen. She felt nauseous and wondered if it because of the narrow, winding road they were hurtling along, leaving Kirkintilloch behind.

She'd never been carsick in her life. She prided herself on it, had judged Andy a few months earlier, when they'd got the CalMac ferry to Islay for a distillery tour and he'd spent the whole time bright green and crawling about the toilet while she stood on the deck, loving the feel of the icy spray on her face.

She noticed the sweet smell again, and as her stomach gave a lurch she realised she had been drugged. He must have touched the brakes as they approached a roundabout and she tipped forward, finally realised what was odd about her viewpoint. She was too high off the ground, on a seat that was straight backed and shallow. They weren't in a car but a van.

A sign flashed by. Lennoxtown. That was where they found that woman a few weeks before. Laura, she thought. Lorna. Lauren. Something like that. She'd been strangled.

He was going to strangle Jade.

Terror clutched at Jade's throat, hammered at her to scream, scratch, jump, but her body was still woozy and slow. She felt trapped, as though she were drowning in herself.

'Stop the car,' she murmured. She wasn't sure if she imagined him pressing on the gas pedal, the burst of speed that sent her stomach lurching. 'I'm gonnae be sick,' she insisted. She looked over at him but his face was in shadow. He was darkness, she thought, a hard, heavy feeling pressing on her throat. Nothing but darkness.

Now, Jade fumbled for her car door handle and half fell out the car, teary with relief as chilly, fresh air filled her lungs. She was vaguely aware of Roddy helping her to her feet. 'I'm okay,' she wheezed. 'I'm so sorry, so sorry about this. I'm fine, honestly.' Her teeth were chattering.

'Just come and sit.'

He led her over to a wee wall bordering someone's front garden. The garden was beautifully tended, bordered with neat beds of geraniums and roses and wee purple ones Jade couldn't identify.

'Looks like this lawn has been clipped with scissors,' she muttered.

'What? Aye, so it does. Are you okay now?'

Jade shrugged. She felt drained, couldn't even bring herself to care what Roddy must think of her. There was something — something about the car, that night. Something she had noticed. Something familiar. She frowned, willing herself to grasp it, but it danced maddeningly just out of reach.

'Are you okay to get back in the car now?' Roddy asked gently. 'Or do you want to find somewhere for a cup of tea or something first?'

'I'm — I'm fine.' Jade forced a smile.

'Maybe I'll drive?'

She didn't want him to, but she didn't have it in her to argue, so she shrugged and allowed him to lead her to the passenger seat. When he clipped his seatbelt on, she looked over, but it wasn't Roddy she saw. The first thing she thought was that he must bleach his hair. It wasn't natural for an adult to have hair that blond.

'JUST TELL ME THAT MUCH,' Cara said. It was an effort to speak around the heavy lump in her throat. 'Is he dead?'

'I don't believe so,' said Alison carefully.

Cara nodded, feeling herself trembling deep within. She clutched onto the desk, mildly surprised that her knees hadn't buckled yet. She was vaguely conscious of Alison approaching. Alison took Cara's arm and gently led her to her chair, then pulled up one of the visitor's seats, perched in it and took Cara's freezing hands between her own.

'Then what?' Cara asked with an exhausted shrug that wracked her whole body. 'If he's not dead, then what?'

Alison clasped her hands together, watched Cara with troubled eyes. 'As I told you in my pre-report briefing yesterday, we were able to recover some trace DNA from the body of Scott Myers. There was a fingerprint and some skin cells on the inside of his wetsuit at the ankle, the same ankle that bears bruising, suggesting it was how he was held underwater.'

Cara nodded, her head still spinning.

'Further skin cells were recovered, again from the wetsuit. There is a flap on the inside of the neck, something to do with insulation. I believe that the killer dragged Scott Myers from the water by the neck of his wetsuit, prior to mutilating the body.'

'Okay,' Cara frowned. 'That is — useful.'

'We ran the samples of course, and they came up with a match.'

'A match?'

'Both the DNA from the skin cells and the fingerprint.'

'We have him on file?' Cara's heart started to thud. 'We know who he is?'

'Cara —'

'That's — it's excellent. Let me call the others back in.'

'Cara.'

Cara caught the note in Alison's voice and sat back down, stared into her friend's eyes, silently pleading.

'Cara, it's Stellan. The DNA and fingerprint we found on the body of Scott Myers is from Stellan.'

7

J ade couldn't make up her mind whether she recognised the two detectives who sat before her or not. For the first six months or so after the attack, she had been interviewed regularly, and a handful of times since, she had approached the police with half-formed memories. After a while, they had all morphed into one, somewhat patronising, well-meaning person who thought she was bonkers.

The woman had introduced herself as DI Samira Shah, and the man Kevin MacGregor, though Jade had forgotten his title or whatever you called it. DI Shah stared impassively as Jade tried to explain why she had come in, but there was a warmth in Kevin's brown eyes that made her feel as though he was sympathetic. Then Jade remembered they were probably doing that good cop/bad cop thing so Jade would feel safe with him while the woman kept her on her toes. Probably she was lovely in real life and he was an arrogant arse.

'Blond hair, tied back in a ponytail, or maybe a bun,' she

said, twisting her hanky in her hands. 'I can't remember exactly. But really blond, the kind of blond you only see on babies.'

Samira and Kevin exchanged a glance, and it occurred to Jade this meant something to them. They knew who he was. That was good news, she reminded herself as a chill washed over her.

'I didn't see him clearly, it was just a — an impression, really. A glimpse.'

'Did he speak at all?'

'I don't — I'm not sure. He must have, but I don't remember.'

'Is there anything else you can tell us about his description?'

'It was mostly the hair I noticed.' She closed her eyes, trying to conjure up the image that had come to her. 'The moon came out from behind a cloud, that's when I saw him.'

'This was when you were in the car?' Samira asked.

'No — no, sorry, I thought that at first, because I saw the glimpse of his face when I was in the car yesterday, but I realised later that the angle didn't make sense. It was a van, I remembered that. He was driving me in a van, but I never saw his face then. It was later. I think it was when I got over the wall. I glanced behind me and the moon came out from behind a cloud and I caught sight of him. It was so quick, all I really saw was his hair. And his nose. He had a really straight nose.'

'Okay Jade, you've done brilliant' said Kevin. 'If it's okay with you, we'd like you to have a chat with a police sketch artist, just see if they can come up with something that looks like him?'

'Based on blond hair and straight nose?'

He smiled kindly. 'You'd be surprised at the wee details they pick up you don't even realise. They're pure amazing.'

'Well I'm happy to give it a go.'

'That's fantastic, thank you. If you could just wait here a minute we'll get somebody along to you, okay?'

'IT'S HIM,' said Samira as soon as Kevin closed the door behind them. There was a strange edge to her voice he couldn't quite identify.

'See what the sketch artist comes up with,' he replied. 'There's plenty blond folk in the world.'

'Now we know why he disappeared that night.'

'Come on Samira, that's an awful leap. You knew Stellan.'

'Sounds like nobody knew Stellan. I always said he was too perfect,' she added as Kevin started down the hallway. 'They're the ones you've got to watch, I'm telling you.'

'Aye, well, let's just —'

'I don't want this to be true,' Samira said, stopping short outside their office. 'Don't think that. I'm just facing facts. We can't let loyalty to Cara get in the way here.'

'I know that,' Kevin replied uncomfortably. 'But there's no need to jump to conclusions yet, either.'

Samira shrugged, her expression hard. 'Do you not think it's weird that a detective chief inspector was right there when Lorna Stewart's sister tried to kill Alec McAvoy, and she just let it happen?'

Kevin stared at her. 'She didnae *let it happen*, she couldn't stop it.'

'How do we know that? Alec can't tell us any different, and nobody saw outside of that wee crew. They would lie for each other. Don't tell me you don't know that too. I'm not saying anything dodgy happened, I'm just saying Cara has been way too deeply involved in this for a long time.'

'And that makes Stellan a murderer? Come on Samira, will ye listen to yourself?'

'Just get that sketch artist and see what they come up with.'

'Don't say anything to Cara yet. Not until we —'

'She's gone,' said Samira. 'Liam put her on indefinite leave first thing this morning.'

THE NIGHT before she went to prison, Greer had sat up in bed in the room she and Lorna used to share, in their parents' house in Kirkintilloch, and read Lorna's blog.

'Try to get your mind off it, pet,' her mum whispered when she came in to get a good night as though she were ten. Greer's mum sat on the bed and stroked Greer's hair back off her face. The feeling of the duvet tightening where her mum sat brought such a strong wave of nostalgia to childhood, to a time when her mum and dad could make everything better, that Greer nearly broke down then and there. Instead, she promised her mum she would get a good night's sleep, and continued reading Lorna's words until dawn broke.

She didn't know what she was looking for in Lorna's blog that night. She must have read it a thousand times by then, discussed it with Ruari a thousand more. She knew it off by heart by now. Even so, she needed to feel close to Lorna that night, and reading her blog was the only way she knew how.

So she read the entire thing, from start to finish. And then she read it again. On her third time through, when light was breaking through their ancient My Little Pony

Curtains, the ones she and Lorna moaned about for their entire teenage years but never quite got around to replacing, she saw it.

Kathleen Connolly.

Lorna had written a post about how she tracked down Kathleen Connolly via one of those nostalgia message boards where folk exchange black-and-white photos of wee boys playing kick the can and one-up each other with stories of psycho shipyard foremen and dancing at Joanna's and the Electric Ballrooms. Kathleen Connolly was a bit of a self-appointed community leader, sternly reminding posters of the rules if they stepped out of line, and she often posted fond memories of her time running the Scouts in the Springburn area in the eighties and nineties.

She had been Alec McAvoy's pack leader. She had stayed with him the night his mother never came to pick him up. When Lorna tracked her down, she told her how they had sat together all evening in the freezing scout hut, even after the electricity and heating automatically went off at eight o'clock. She explained how she had tried to distract the solemn wee boy by challenging him to find candles and matches, tried to pretend it was all a scout challenge, as the hours ticked by and they both knew that Elaine wasn't coming.

At about ten o'clock, she decided that an eleven year old needed to be in bed, so she took him home with her, reasoning she could use her house phone to ring round some of Elaine's neighbours to see if anyone knew what had happened. Nobody did, so she made up a bed on her couch. The next morning, he didn't say a word as she gave him tea and toast then walked him round the corner to school. The moment she spotted the police car parked haphazardly in front of the playground, she knew.

When Lorna emailed her twenty years later, Kathleen Connolly had invited her to visit the village of Kilmacolm where she now lived with her daughter and son-in-law. When Lorna arrived, Kathleen greeted her with a stern telling-off for being yet another muckraking journalist trying to make cash from a tragedy. Lorna had been mortified, had almost given up on the project there and then, and the first time Greer read that post she had felt a flash of gratitude to Kathleen Connolly. If only Lorna had stuck to her guns and abandoned the whole thing, she might never have met Alec McAvoy.

But that night, the night before she went to prison, Greer noticed something else.

Connolly.

Kilmacolm.

Paige Connolly, the woman Alec had manipulated to try to murder Amy in prison, had lived in Kilmacolm. A quick online search that morning confirmed that Paige Connolly was Kathleen Connolly's niece.

Greer knew then that they had barely scratched the surface of Alec's dark and tangled sphere. It was bigger than Lorna, bigger than Elaine MacPherson, bigger even than the Dancing Girl murders, she thought, as she heard the kettle boiling downstairs and her mum and dad talking in muted voices. Greer had to finish what Lorna had started.

Kathleen Connolly was precisely as Lorna had described her, Greer thought now, as she caught sight of her speaking sternly to the warden who attempted to point her in Greer's direction. 'I am quite capable of identifying the woman myself,' her imperious voice rang clearly out even amongst the chaos of the visitors' hall. 'There are plenty of photographs of her on the internet, thank you very much.'

She was a diminutive woman, with a ramrod straight

posture and steel-grey hair pulled into a severe ballet bun. She wore a corduroy blazer and black leggings tucked into gleaming riding boots, and strode through the visitors' hall as though she were royalty inspecting thoroughbreds at Ascot.

Christ, here we go, thought Greer as Kathleen took her seat at Greer's wee table and looked her up and down. Greer suddenly felt like a naughty schoolgirl called in to the head-mistresses office. She shifted under Kathleen's scrutiny, wishing she'd done something to her hair other than shoved it in a messy ponytail, annoyed with herself for caring what this snobby wee woman thought of her.

'I treated your sister terribly when she came to visit me,' Kathleen Connolly stated suddenly. 'I was intending to write to her to apologise when I read of her death, I am so very sorry.'

'Thank you,' Greer stammered, slightly thrown by the unexpected turn 'Do you know — what happened? Why she was murdered?'

Kathleen nodded. 'I have been following the case ever since, even before Paige's involvement. I remember Alec well.

'I wish I could tell you that I suspected something about the boys, but I didn't. Alec was on the quiet, serious side, but I always put that down to a chaotic home life. His mother tried her best, as far as I could see, she was just a topsy-turvy sort of person and happened to have a little boy who desperately needed order. I wasn't surprised when I read he had gone in to the law. He always had a very keen sense of justice.' She smiled briefly, a kindness that brought a sudden lump to Greer's thoat dancing in her eyes. 'Such as that was, of course.'

'Was your niece involved in the Scouts at all?'

'Not officially, it was boys only. I hear they mix them up these days, which strikes me as a sensible idea. I used to take care of Paige a lot back then — her mother is my much younger half-sister, you see. I was retired and my own children were grown, but Paige's mother was still working and struggling for childcare. So yes, I sometimes had to bring her along when I ran a meeting, I would set her up in a corner of the hall with colouring books or comics and a cup of hot squash. And yes, I believe that is her connection to Alec, at least the origins of it. It's safe to say they would not have moved in the same circles as adults.'

'Did you know that they had kept in touch all these years?'

'No. We knew very little of her life, and know even less now.' Kathleen smiled a tight, sad smile. 'I suppose it won't surprise you to hear she was always a difficult girl. As I am sure you are aware, Paige was badly injured in a fight when she tried to attack Amy Kerr, and she has barely spoken since then.

'But even before, she refused to say a word to anyone in the family about what had happened. She's always been unusual, I suppose the word is, with a wild and often troubling imagination, angry at the world since birth.' Kathleen took a shaky breath and fumbled in her pillbox handbag for a cotton hanky. 'But she had love, she was taken care of. I don't think any of us could have stopped her becoming what she did, that's what frightens me.'

'Would Paige have known Elaine, Alec's mum, at all?'

Kathleen shook her head. 'She may have seen her when she picked Alec up from time to time, but they never spoke, as far as I am aware. I can't see why they would have, Paige was just a little girl. She couldn't have had anything to do with Elaine's murder, if that's what you are asking. She was six years old at the time.'

'I know,' said Greer. 'I'm just trying to build a picture of it all to try to —' She shrugged. 'I think my sister knew more than we do right now. I'm just trying to find out what.'

'I would be happy to help if only I can,' Kathleen said, 'but I don't believe Paige is the connection you are looking for. She was there, but she only a wee girl. At the time, they barely noticed her. She wasn't in their gang.'

'What gang?'

'The gang of three, we used to call them. You know the old nursery rhyme *Three Wee Craws*? A cold and frosty morning, and all that? Elaine would sing *three wee boys* as they all piled into her car.'

WHEN CARA BOUGHT the Bearsden house, she'd thought the electric gates at the bottom of the gravel drive were impossibly pretentious, and figured she would never bother to close them. Her nieces soon put paid to that.

They loved announcing themselves on the intercom like a butler in *Downton Abbey*. 'It's Princess Ayla and Lady Jessa here,' they'd giggle, and if they arrived to find the gates open they were bereft. So Cara made sure they were always closed for the girls, and even though they were teenagers now, they still loved to announce they were here to take tea with Her Ladyship.

Never had Cara been so grateful for her nieces' daftness than that morning, when she pulled into her cul-de-sac to find a gaggle of press cluttering up the pavement outside the gates. They couldn't swarm her property in any case, but it made her feel slightly better, as she nosed through the hurricane of flashes, to know that she would soon be able to press a button to swing the gates in their faces. Even in the car, the firework display of cracking flashbulbs jolted, the rat-a-tat of shutters pounded in her ears like artillery fire as photographers jostled to get that one shot of her looking evil, defeated, terrified, cruel.

'Cara! Cara — DCI Boyle! This way — 'mon hen, gies the shot and we can all go hame. Cara — gonnae jist look this way a minute —'

Cara stared straight ahead, grateful that she had years of practice perfecting her poker face, though aware that there was no expression a digital camera couldn't capture in a microsecond. She might as well just snarl at them and be done with it.

'Cara, how could you not have known your husband was a killer? Is it no' yer joab tae know that kind of thing?'

'Couldn't you tell he was a monster, Cara?'

'How could you not know?'

Finally the car made it through the scrum and the gates swung shut. She killed the engine in front of her door, closed her eyes, steeling herself against the explosion of flashbulbs. They were just shouting the cruelest thing they could to try to make her crack for a juicy picture. She knew that. But suddenly, she couldn't bear to hear it. She froze, her hand on the door handle, trying desperately to summon the last vestiges of her courage to make it across two metres of gravel.

Stellan had once persuaded her to skate on the frozen waters of Lake Mälaren outside his childhood home on Ekerö, and every second she had been so tense her jaw ached for days afterwards, steeling herself for that first crack to echo through the still, icy air. That's how she felt now. Her composure was like the fragile, almost preternatural whiteness that wound its way through Stockholm's commuter belt, and all she could do was brace herself for the crack.

'Cara?'

She heard the soft tap on the driver's window and jumped, ready to tear the head off whatever reporter had had the temerity to broach the line of her property, but it was Ruari. He was holding out a picnic blanket ready to protect her. She glanced up and saw Alison holding the front door open, Amy hovering just inside.

That was when she burst into tears.

'THIS IS THEM?' asked Lauren.

The glorified cupboard in the basement of the station could barely fit both her and Kevin. It was dimly lit, with a single fluorescent strip on the ceiling that made Lauren fully expect a migraine. Two of the walls were dominated with dusty bookshelves and a third was entirely taken up with a whiteboard, on which seventeen photos were tacked. A yellowing lineup for a long-ago netball tournament was pinned to the fourth wall next to the door. There was a small desk shoved in a corner, and two metal fold out chairs.

Lauren had already figured out that there was no angle at which she could sit without her knees jamming against a wall or the desk.

'This is them,' Kevin muttered with a nod, handing Lauren her tea. 'What kinda weirdo doesn't take milk?'

'This kind of weirdo,' she replied with a grin, pointing a thumb at herself.

'Are you that intolerant thingmy?'

'Nah, just don't like milk in tea. I like ice cream okay. If I'd been in Crowded Room would you have me on the wall for not taking milk in my tea?'

'Aye, I'd have you at the top,' Kevin said. He sat next to Lauren and jiggled the mouse to wake up the ancient desktop computer. 'I've goat the whole database on here, but I like seeing it all big up there on the wall. Must've caught that off Cara.'

'Do you think Cara's okay?' Lauren asked.

'No, I do not.'

'Did you ever meet Stellan?'

'Aye, once or twice.'

'What did you think?'

Kevin shrugged. 'Ach, I thought Alec McAvoy wis a great guy mentoring me. What do I know?'

'But that's exactly it — you spent more time with McAvoy than most people. Did Stellan — I don't know, remind you of him in some way? Knowing all we know now, I mean.'

Kevin thought a moment, dipped a biscuit in his tea. 'I don't think it works quite like that. McAvoy worked alongside some of the top folk in criminal justice. He was in the Lord Advocate's office every week, consulted with police most days, and not a single soul spotted what he was. A few have come out now and said they always thought he was a funny one, but that's easy to do now. Or look at Amy — she dedicated her life tae understanding the mind of a killer, and here she was washing one of their pants the whole time.'

'So what's the point of this?' Lauren demanded, gesturing to the seventeen faces on the wall in front of them.

'Most likely an exercise in futility,' Kevin replied with a rueful grin.

'Is it all futile?' Lauren blurted. 'Everything we do? If we can't stop these things happening, what's the point?'

'Nobody can stop bad things happening, that's not what

we're here for,' Kevin said, leaning back in his chair with a yawn. 'It's more about managing. Preventing second and third crimes, avoiding the worst case scenario.

'That's the point of this project,' he added, nodding towards the wall. 'You know, by the way, it's not entirely legit? The official version is that it's just about following up on everybody that was involved in the app to check what they knew, get a better sense of who it targeted, all that kind of thing.'

'My sister Emma was on Crowded Room,' Lauren said. 'Before she went travelling.'

Kevin nodded. 'Aye, I know. I talked to her. She was one of the real ones just lookin' for the boaby.'

'Well that's good to hear,' Lauren grinned dryly. 'So who are these seventeen?'

There were fourteen men and three women on the wall. The photos were unremarkable, mostly standard dating app headshots, cropped out of group pictures. A few were show-offy, featuring ski lifts or surfboards. One was a dog, another an exceptionally well-defined torso. Next to each photo was a series of numbers.

'The basic idea behind profiling is that folk are predictable. Certain circumstances and personality traits result in certain behaviours. It's not, like, psychic stuff, it's patterns. Behaviours get repeated and time and time again they result in crimes. It's surprisingly consistent. We're all creatures of habit and none of us is quite as staggeringly unique as we'd like to think.'

'Do you mean like the way they talk about the stages of a breakup?' asked Lauren with a frown. 'All my pals, even though we're really different, we all go through the same crying/psycho/goddess-rising-from-the-ashes cycle.'

'Aye, exactly, that is a good comparison. Obviously every

break up is different, but you're right, we all go through more or less the same set of emotions. And similarly, it's basically the same process that builds somebody towards serial killing.

'So normally, we have to work in reverse. We look at a crime scene and pick out elements that could speak to the personality or lifestyle or background of the offender and use that information to help catch him or her.

'Here —' he pointed to the wall. 'It's the opposite. We have a group of people, and maybe one of them, maybe more, is potentially a serial killer.'

'But you can't do anything unless they commit a crime.'

'Aye, well, no. That's the unofficial bit. These seventeen have been pulled out because they meet enough of the criteria that could suggest they have it in them. That's what the numbers are — I don't want to write the actual things in case anybody happens to poke their nose in here one day. Doesnae mean any of them are ever going to do a thing, loads of us meet the criteria and live our lives without murdering a single soul — but then these folk also signed up to a website that Alec McAvoy was using to trawl for puppets.

'This one, for example —' He pointed to a photo of a handsome guy frowning moodily at the camera, his thick brown hair artfully ruffled. 'When I looked into him, I found out he had a long term girlfriend. Could just be your typical love rat looking for a bit on the side, or maybe he was there for different reasons altogether.'

'He looks like a love rat,' Lauren said, wrinkling her nose. 'If I came from the last century and used words like love rat, in any case.'

Kevin laughed. 'Aye, well, my geriatric status aside, we've

no way of knowing if McAvoy had his eye on any of them, but that's why I have my eye on them.'

'Is that legal?' Lauren asked.

'If it could stop somebody else being murdered by these bastards, I don't give a fuck.'

'What can you actually do, though?'

'I keep an eye,' Kevin shrugged. 'Relationship status, employment status — big life changes like divorce or redundancy can push folk with the potential over the edge. There's somebody that helps me, outside the force. If a murder happens, we'd know right away if any of them were nearby, for example — and if so, we might just manage to get to them before the next one.'

'I don't recognise any of these faces. Are any of them in the frame for Bobby O'Brien or Scott Myers?'

Kevin shook his head. 'Naw.' He sighed. 'That's why this might well be an exercise in futility. Maybe they're all just unfortunate buggers who were trying to get laid.' He frowned suddenly.

'If that's the case they'll never know you had your eye on them,' Lauren shrugged, finishing her tea. 'No harm, no foul.'

'Oh fuck.'

'What?'

'Him.' Kevin got up, approached the wall, stared at one of the photos. 'Love rat. It was him. At Bobby's funeral.'

'WHAT DID YOU JUST DO?' Jade asked, wiping sweat from her brow. Hannah kneeled on the mat, trying to get her breath back. 'You gave ground. You let me in.'

From the floor, Hannah gave her a shaky finger and Jade laughed. 'If this was real life, you'd be dead.'

'Ach I would not, I'd just phone the police.'

'Not if you'd swung your bag in his face and it had your phone in it.'

'I suppose that's true.'

Hannah beckoned to Jade to sit down too. 'I need to catch my breath a minute.'

Jade sat next to her, took a sip of her water. Shouts and squeaks of trainers echoed off the bare concrete walls of the warehouse-like gym. A handful of pairs were sparring on other mats, and at the far end, a yoga for boxing class was stretching into a sideways star pose.

'Smacking him in the face with your bag was genius, by the way. I don't think I would ever have thought of that.'

Jade shrugged, watching the yoga class. 'Not really. It was a risk. I gave ground when he yanked the strap and I stumbled. It was sheer luck he never managed to grab me.'

'Funny how that's one of the things you remember. You remember that, you remember getting over the wall and hitting your head, and then the next morning when that wee shower of Neds picked you up. Is that it?'

Jade shrugged again. One of the yogis fell over and burst out laughing. Someone somewhere blew a whistle to signal the beginning of a spar. Jade could feel Hannah's eyes on her. 'I've remembered being in the car. Bits of it, anyway.'

'Because of this pal of Ruari's?'

'Dunno. Yeah, I think so. She hypnotised me. I was dead against it, but I don't know — she gets your trust somehow. I don't really remember what happened when I was, you know, under. I vaguely remember her voice and stuff, but not any of the memories. She said we would discuss what I told her next time, when it wasn't so overwhelming. But that afternoon — mind I told you about that guy that chatted me up at the café? I was feeling all, take life by the horns, and I texted him to see if he wanted to come kayaking.'

'Brilliant, Jade. Is he nice?'

'Well the thing is, on the way home, I had an attack and it came with a kind of flashback. I remembered being in the car with the attacker. He picked me up when I was on my way back from getting a takeaway the night Andy left. I saw what he looked like.'

'What?' Hannah squeezed her hand, her voice laced with shock. 'Are you okay? Have you told the police?'

Jade nodded. 'I went this morning.' A heavy feeling had settled over her that she didn't understand. This was great. Remembering him was a relief. It was the beginning of the end. 'I think they recognised the description. I think they know who he is.'

'Jade, this is huge. I'm so happy for you. Wait — is it not good?' Hannah asked, giving Jade a searching look.

'I don't know what's up with me,' Jade sighed. 'I feel weird and I don't know why. It is good. It's brilliant.'

'Maybe you just need to process it a bit. You might just be wobbly because it's such a big thing after so long.'

'Aye maybe. 'Mon let's go for another wee round.'

Jade got up, took another gulp of water and her stomach fell to her knees. *Fuck's sake,* she growled to herself. Would there never not be a time her heart clutched at the sight of that skinny malinky long legs?

'Don't bother to say hello to him,' Hannah said quickly, wrinkling her nose at the sight of Andy battering the hell out of a punching bag.

'How can I not? I've shown up at his front door begging him to reconsider our breakup every bloody second week for two years.'

'That's not your fault and he should know that.'

'He does.'

'Why are you sticking up for him?'

'I'm not. Hannah, what are you on about? Obviously I have to say hello if he sees us.'

'Well he's not yet.'

'No. I know,' Jade muttered, watching Andy's shoulders ripple as he battered the punching bag, sweat dripping down his neck.

'Thought you wanted to go another round,' Hannah said impatiently.

'Naw. Let's call it a day.'

'Have you got time for a wee glass of wine?' Hannah persisted. 'Or why don't you come to ours for dinner? Ruari's out the night.'

Jade made a face. 'Thanks, but I'll maybe just —'

'Jade, don't do this,' Hannah snapped, and Jade stared at her in surprise.

'Do what?'

'You always go to pieces when you see him, and you are so much better than it.'

'Well can you blame me?' Jade demanded. 'Seeing as how —'

'No. Not since the break up and what happened and everything. It's nothing to do with that. It's been since the minute you met him. See that night in the Record Factory? Do you know how many times I've kicked myself for not insisting we went to Ashton Lane?'

'I know I abandoned you a bit when we were together,' Jade said uncomfortably. 'But doesn't everyone do that a bit when they're first with someone? The whole honeymoon thing.'

'I've not abandoned you since I've been with Ruari.'

'Aye but I'm a nutcase, remember?' Jade grinned, 'if you

abandon me I might go running up Sauchiehall Street with my skirt over my head or something.'

Hannah's face remained impassive and Jade's smile faded. A cheer went up, echoed off the high ceiling, as somebody got their partner on the ground. The yoga class wobbled in varying versions of crows pose.

'He's a waste of space,' Hannah shrugged finally. 'I'm sorry, but he is. He was never worth a tenth of you, and I just wish you could see that.'

'Aye, well,' said Jade, slipping her arm through Hannah's as they made their way to the changing rooms, 'you always did have an exceptionally high opinion of me.'

THERE HAD BEEN a moment when Cara worried that now she'd started crying she'd never stop. All the clichés about the dam breaking were true, it seemed. Alison and Ruari led her gently into the living room where she curled up on one of the cold Chesterfields and howled. Alison sat next to her and stroked her hair, handed her hankies, while Ruari and Amy waited on the other couch.

Finally the storm blew itself out and Cara began to feel that she could breathe again. Slowly she sat up, snuffling and wiping her nose and face with one of the sodden hankies. 'Well that's a bit better,' she muttered though a shaky smile.

'These are from Moira,' Amy said, handing over a brown paper bag splattered with promising grease spots. 'Ruari is putting the kettle on.'

'First tell me if there is any way the DNA you found could be wrong,' Cara said to Alison. 'Misplaced, mixed up, anything. Is there any possibility? I know the answer, but I need to hear you say it right now.'

Ruari silently handed round tea in her good china, and Cara was grateful for its warmth in her hands. She opened the bag of home made millionaires shortbread, and picked at a piece, feeling the sugar rush hit her almost instantly. Alison thought for a long time before she answered.

'Yes,' she said finally, with a helpless sigh. 'There's always a possibility. I handled it myself, I do know that there's been no mistake on our end, it's not been contaminated or anything like that, but there are other explanations. You know that as well as I do, Cara. Forensic evidence isn't some magical divining rod, whatever crime dramas would have us believe. It's just stuff that's there, it's all open to interpretation.'

'I know it doesn't mean he killed anyone, but it does mean he was there. Involved, connected somehow.'

'Could Stellan have worn the wetsuit at some point?' Ruari asked.

'Weirder things have happened. I once heard a story about a guy who was almost convicted of rape because his girlfriend had lent a pair of jeans to a friend.' Alison said. 'The girlfriend had worn the jeans after sex with him, then the friend was wearing them when she was raped. A microscopic trace of the boyfriend's semen was found on the jeans, while the rapist wore a condom. No single piece of evidence is conclusive proof of anything. Has Stellan got a wetsuit?'

'He's with the killer. He is connected to the killer.' said Cara, more shortly than she intended. Her next words caught in her throat but she forced them out. 'Or he is the killer.'

'We know he's not,' Ruari said quickly, and Cara made herself shake her head.

'We don't. We can't close our minds to anything right

now. It won't help Stellan. He has a scuba diving license. He trained in Thailand the holiday when we met, and he's kept it up since. There's shipwrecks around the Hebrides he's explored, and Loch Fyne, I think. Samira must be coming to interview me, I'll give her all the information.' Cara was vaguely aware that she sounded like a robot. She felt woozy. All she wanted to do was close her eyes and sleep for a week.

'I think I know who he's with,' blurted Amy. 'That's what I came to say.' She put her tea down, got up, as though she couldn't sit still any longer.

They had shut the curtains to avoid the press even getting a glimpse of movement that would set them off, and Amy stood in front of the fireplace, her face almost hidden in the shadows. Cara shivered. Amy rubbed her forehead. 'I don't really know where to start. I suspected when I saw how the bodies were posed, but —'

'How did you know about how the bodies were posed?' Cara snapped, then remembered. Amy had been there.

'I was running in Victoria Park last week. I was a few metres from stumbling across the body myself when a dog walker just in front of me started screaming. Then on Sunday I was running on Conic when the swimmer was found.'

'Is it a coincidence?' Cara asked.

Amy hesitated. 'Nobody has heard from Stuart in more than two years.'

'Your husband Stuart?'

'The very one.'

Amy fell silent a few moments. From outside, they heard a van door slam. The last of the media must have given up. Finally, Amy spoke again.

'Every few months ever since he was sentenced, Stuart

has tried to contact me somehow. Whether via the press, a direct phone call or letter, or through his lawyers — there would be some request, some promise to give details about where they could find another body if only his darling wife would visit him. The first few times, I spoke to his lawyers about what I should do. If there was any possibility some poor woman's family could be put out of the misery of wondering and be allowed to grieve, then of course I would visit him.

'But the lawyers believed that Stuart had told the FBI everything there was to tell and that he was just playing games, so I ignored him, but the requests didn't stop. I'm fairly sure the press conference announcing I was the real monster was him just upping the stakes to get my attention.'

'I wondered if it was related to Alec,' Ruari said. 'It's weird how Stuart accused you of doing to him exactly what Alec did to his puppets.'

'Could have been both,' Amy shrugged. 'Could have been Stuart's twisted way of letting us know he knew what Alec was doing. He always did like riddles.'

'Has he been in touch with his lawyers during this time?' asked Alison. 'I thought there was some talk of an appeal?'

Amy shook her head. 'That was just press speculation. I went to visit Stuart, about a year ago.

'We weren't going to get any answers from Alec, and I persuaded myself that talking to Stuart in person was worth a shot. I contacted the lawyers, arranged for a visiting order, got on a flight to Houston, but when I arrived, the prison informed me he was ill. Strep throat. High fever, severely dehydrated, taken to hospital. They said he was unable to see anyone.

'I hung around for a few days, then I realised that this was exactly what he would do if I finally gave in and got a visiting order. He was letting me know he could still control whether or not he saw me. So I got the next plane home, but I still had this nagging feeling that he might just have something to tell me. A couple of months later I contacted the lawyers again, asked to arrange some kind of web call. Again, it was all approved and arranged, and cancelled at the last minute. Every few months since then, same thing.'

'You think he's still mucking you about?'

'Could well be,' Amy said with a nod. 'It would be completely in character for him. But —' She sighed. 'I don't know.' She gave a cynical grin. 'Call it wifely intuition. Better late than never. I've just had this niggling feeling that something isn't right.'

'And what your client told you today confirmed that?'

'It confirmed something I suspected since I came across that poor bugger in Victoria Park last week. To answer your question, no, I don't believe it's a coincidence I just so happened to be out jogging where these bodies are showing up. How could it be?' Amy finally turned to look at Cara, a quiet terror in her eyes.

'I think Stuart escaped from prison two years ago. I think he is killing these men and leaving the bodies for me.'

'Amy — listen to yourself. How does someone escape from prison — from death row?' demanded Ruari. 'You think they just mislaid him somehow?'

'I don't know,' she said. 'I just know that —'

'Not to mention get all the way to Scotland without a passport,' he continued. 'You think he just strolled through airport security and talked his way on a plane? Or do you think he swam?'

'I don't know. I just know that —'

'This is absurd,' Ruari insisted, staring around at them in horror.

'She described him.'

'What?'

'Jade. I put her under hypnosis today and she described Stuart to a T. It was him that attacked her. He attacked her the night we caught Alec.'

8

'This isn't easy,' Liam said. He stood with his hands in his pockets at the front of the incident room.

The room was packed, Lauren noted sourly. Everyone and anyone who could possibly claim a tenuous link to the investigation had inserted themselves. Her dad was at the front too, just to the right of Liam, balancing his notebook against the arm of his wheelchair as he took notes. At least he had a right to be here, Lauren thought, as she noticed a couple of DIs from a whole other division leaning against desks, their arms crossed, expressions solemn.

'Many of us knew Stellan, and even those that didn't will find this difficult simply because he was so close to one of us. That is quite understandable, I am struggling with it a fair bit myself. If anybody feels uncomfortable with this development, or as though they would not be able to carry out their duties without undue stress, then I ask you to privately have a word with myself, or Iain McNabb if you prefer.

'It won't count against you in any way, we will just rearrange the team's responsibilities as necessary, no questions asked.' He paused then, as though half expecting a round of applause for his benevolence.

'As difficult as it is for us to accept, the case against Stellan Åstrand is compelling. This morning, the procurator fiscal issued a warrant for his arrest, in connection with the murders of Bobby O'Brien and Scott Myers and for the attempted murder of Jade McFadyen.

'Of course as everyone is aware, the man has been missing for just over two years now, so I don't expect any of you to magic him out of thin air. But that's — that's as things stand now. Stellan Åstrand is our man and we will do everything in our power to find him and bring him in. Thank you.'

Liam nodded, a curiously nervous gesture, hesitated a moment as though wondering if he should say more, then turned and walked sharply out of the room. The moment the door closed behind him, a babble of shocked chatter broke out. Lauren heard someone start to recount the story of arm wrestling with Stellan at some Christmas drinks party, and slipped from the room in disgust.

She had a Skype call arranged with Scott Myers' sister in Vancouver for 9am her time, and was terrified she would miscount the time difference and miss it. She decided to stay near her laptop and signed into Skype for the next few hours just to be on the safe side.

She knew that DNA evidence against Stellan was compelling, there was no two ways about that, she thought as she leaned back in her desk chair, coffee cup in hand. She had seen the sketch the artist came up with after consulting with Jade McFadyen, and like everyone else in the department, recognised Stellan instantly.

Her dad, a longtime case manager, was fond of holding forth at great length on his opinion of coppers' hunches.

'They like to think they're bloody Mystic Meg,' he'd chortle over dinner as Lauren and her sisters exchanged glances and wondered just how long he'd bang on for this time. 'But it all comes down to understanding the evidence. Nothing fancier than that. They love claiming they 'just knew' this lead or that would pan out, but it was nothing but picking up on a piece of evidence their brain hadn't quite consciously processed. I'm telling yous here and now, there's no such bloody thing as a hunch.'

'Thank you for coming to my Ted talk,' Emma would whisper under her breath and the sisters would snigger as their mum gave them a warning look over a mountain of mashed potatoes.

If her dad was right, Lauren didn't have a hunch that Stellan was innocent, she knew it, somehow, subconsciously. She just had to figure out how.

'Oh it's like 4am here,' Sheana Myers said an hour or two later when Lauren pointed out that it was pitch dark behind Sheana's picture windows. 'But I can't sleep. I haven't slept, since — since Sunday, when we got the call that — I guess that's normal. Except that nothing about his is normal.'

She was talking too fast, Lauren thought, her eyes unnaturally wide, darting to and fro. 'My parents are in the air right now, heading for Scotland. They're going to bring his — him. They're going to bring him home, for the funeral. It's Saturday. There's so many people coming,' she added, her eyes shining with unshed tears. 'It's gonna be crazy.'

Lauren finally managed to to bring the conversation round to the list she had emailed Sheana to put together, of anybody she could remember him mentioning in Glasgow. Her hunch-that-couldn't-be-a-hunch was that there was some connection they hadn't come across yet. Some spark that would begin to assemble the moving parts of the investigation into a pattern that would start to make sense. A few minutes later, there it was.

'It was, like two, two-and-a-half years ago, maybe?' Sheana was saying. 'It was right before he climbed the Matterhorn. I remember thinking it was a waste of money, Scott was workout-obsessed since he was a teen and I really didn't think there was much a personal trainer could tell him he wouldn't know already, but he said she was great. I don't remember the exact details, but he worked out with her for a couple weeks, got to be good buddies, but then her boyfriend got jealous and she passed him onto another trainer. I don't think it was any huge deal, but —'

'What was her name, the trainer?'

'That I do remember. Jade somebody-or-other. I remember because I thought it was a really pretty name.'

STELLAN HAD COME ACROSS AN OLD, tapestry-type woven mat rolled up in a cupboard the day before, pinned it to the washing line behind the bothy and painstakingly battered the worst of the dust and muck from it. Over the months he had got used to doing yoga directly on the soft grass or heather or bracken outside of wherever they were, but he was looking forward to getting to do a headstand on a slightly firmer surface.

Now, he held the heavy oak door open with the mat tucked under his arm, and the dog trotted out after him. She was a mutt, a gloriously ugly abomination of affection and snuffles and probably a bit of terrier, and she knew to stay silent until they were out of earshot.

The early morning sun twinkled on the dew as Stellan took a deep breath of fresh air, and drank in soothing view. Deep green mountains rolling gently as far as the eye could see, draped with the morning mist, faded into purple on the horizon. Far below he could just glimpse the twinkle of water, though he couldn't tell whether it was a river or the tip of a loch. Loch Lomond tapered to a narrow end before drifting into the River Falloch. Stellan tried not to let himself hope that was what he could see. If he was in sight of Loch Lomond then he was the closest to Cara he had been in two years.

The bothy was a tiny white stone cottage, no more than a cramped room inside, dominated by a large fireplace caked with centuries of grime and smoke. A cracked sink and single gas hob formed the kitchen, and the privy was outdoors and the stuff of nightmares. The two narrow windows on the back wall were warped and cracked, and left the cottage shadowy even on the brightest of days. As Stellan hiked up the steep verge that rose behind the cottage, he could hear snores emanating from within.

A few metres above the cottage, there was a small, flat patch of grass that was reasonably free of rocks. When Stellan stumbled across it the day before, he had asked the dog if she agreed it had once been a lookout point, where villagers took turns keeping an eye out for approaching Redcoats. She had cocked her head to one side and wagged her tail, which Stellan took as a yes.

In several of the bothies, caravans and holiday cottages they had squatted in over the months, Stellan had come across small bookcases stuffed with yellowing paperbacks. He had read tomes of Scottish history, Highland romances filled with strapping warriors and lusty maidens whose bosoms had a habit of escaping their corsets with alacrity, and adventures in which plucky teenagers outwitted criminal masterminds.

In the early mornings, when he finally heard the snores

and knew he could relax for a few hours, Stellan would close his eyes and imagine telling Cara about the story he had spent the night reading by candlelight. He would hear her laugh as he earnestly described a forbidden romance with the swarthy laird of the next village, and critiqued the realism of the enthusiasm with which the characters whipped their tartans off in the land of nettles and midges.

'If it were my only chance to be with you before your father had me hung, drawn and quartered I would do it,' he would picture explaining, putting on the serious face that always had her helpless with giggles, 'but I would be a little bit afraid and perhaps only uncover the most necessary body parts.'

Sometimes he wrote these imaginary conversations with Cara in the flimsy wirebound notebook he had taken from the first cottage. It had been placed next to the old fashioned rotary phone in the hallway, evidently intended for messages. Stellan assuaged his guilt at the theft by reminding himself that absolutely nobody would ever phone the landline of the holiday cottage their friends were staying at.

Now, Stellan arranged the mat just how he wanted it, placed his forearms and flipped nimbly into a headstand. He could smell the sweetness of the Highland air, the bite of the wind that made him feel alert, the pleasure of his feet reaching to the sky, the blood rushing to his head. He allowed himself a moment of something approaching joy.

Out of the corner of his eye, he spotted an osprey circling the valley below. As he watched the magnificent bird drift powerfully on the wind, he was filled with gratitude that he existed and got to share the world with that mighty creature. He let his feet fall and he drew back into child's pose, smelling the earth and dew beneath his face.

He was alive, he was surviving, and any day now Cara would find him.

'IT'S NOTHING CERTAIN,' said Jack, poking his head around Alison's office door. She looked exhausted, he thought. She pulled off her reading glasses to frown at him. He knew that she had spent the night at Cara's, and suspected she hadn't had a wink of sleep.

'What is it?'

'The two bits of the wetsuit where we found the skin cells and the fingerprint.'

'The left ankle and the back of the neck.'

'Aye, right. Well, they've both been patched.'

Alison frowned. 'How do you mean, patched?'

'Mended. It's quite an old wetsuit. There was a wee tear at the ankle which has some fairly old traces of Myers' blood in the fibre, I would say he'd caught his leg on something, barbed wire maybe, once upon a time. The neck isn't a full hole, it's just worn a bit thin, and Scott Myers, or somebody, has reinforced it with a patch.

'There's nothing unusual about that, you get this wee kit, with a gel thing that seals the patch in so the suit is still waterproof. But both these repairs were done quite recently and I think at the same time'

'And Stellan's skin cells and the fingerprint were on the patches, not the suit itself?'

Jack nodded. 'There are a couple of other wee mends, like I say, it's a pretty crappy old suit. There's nothing but traces of Scott Myers on any of the older patches. The two patches where we found Stellan's DNA are the only two new ones.'

'What are the patches made of? Do they come with this kit?'

'They do, but they're just the same fabric as a wetsuit —'

'So they could come from another wetsuit — one Stellan has worn?'

Jack nodded. 'It's possible,' he said carefully.

'Cara said Stellan dives. Get round to hers and find out if he has a wetsuit, and find out if it's still there.'

JADE SPAN on her left foot and ducked, nimbly slipping out of Andy's reach. She sensed him lunging for her, but he was clumsy, off balance, and from her lower vantage point she rammed her shoulder into his hip and he staggered, fell to the ground.

'Nice Jade, use that advantage —'

Jade barely heard the words echoing against the high ceiling of the gym. Her entire focus was on Andy. He was sitting up, his hands guarding his chest as he tried to scrabble back enough to be able to get to his feet. Jade sharply swiped his hands out the way as she stepped deep between his legs, pressed the heel of her her hand against his sternum and held him on the ground. Andy tried to sit up against her hand, his face contorted into a grimace — Jade gritted her teeth to keep the pressure on as she straddled his left leg, prepared for her next move —

'Rookie mistake Andy, you're asking her to break your rib —'

Andy drew his knees back to his chest and Jade felt him prepare to kick her from below — she quickly shoved his right knee with her left hand, forcing his leg to straighten as she scrabbled round to cover his chest with hers.

'Ugly Jade, but it worked — three, two — Andy, you're down —'

But Andy rolled swiftly, knocking Jade off balance and suddenly she was on her back, winded — her vision filled with blackness and she saw a face lunging at her in the darkness. *Not Andy — the blond man — she moaned, scrabbled away over rocks and icy dew, her heart thudding sharply — she felt her bag strap between her fingers and swung wildly, feeling the satisfying thud of its weight colliding with his nose as he yowled in pain — then she frowned —*

'Wait — stop —'

Andy was on top of her, pinning her to the ground —

'Andy, she said stop —'

Jade drew back, holding up a hand as she desperately tried to grab what she had glimpsed in the darkness. Something wasn't right, something jarred — but it danced just out of reach as she felt Andy grab her hand, haul her up.

'You okay, Jade? Sorry, pet, I thought —'

'I'm fine,' she muttered, as they padded across the mats towards the changing rooms. She shoved her sweaty fringe off her forehead, knowing it would now be sticking up in the fetching manner of an eighties rock star. 'Sorry, I just got distracted a second. Nice one, by the way. Your technique is getting there, you just need to work on your speed. Snappy reactions. Don't think, trust your instincts.'

Andy didn't smile. He stared at her with concern-filled eyes and Jade only just resisted rolling hers.

'But I mean, are you okay?' he asked softly.

'I know we split up two years ago, if that's what you mean.'

'I didn't mean that.'

'Then what did you mean?' she said sharply. He was staring at her with that unrelenting eye contact that used to make her think he was fascinated by her. Jade shifted under his scrutiny, wishing the gym wasn't so quiet all of a sudden. She'd been sparring with the punching bag, a satisfying series of tight, powerful jabs, enjoying the satisfying sensation of thirty kilos of leather and sand trembling beneath her, when she caught sight of Andy hovering nearby out of the corner of her eye.

'Do you come here often?' he'd grinned, and she laughed. The hours she spent here battering the hell out of punching bags were one of the things they had fought about. 'I never expected to see you here twice in one week.'

He'd shrugged. 'Maybe I'm finally getting what you were banging on about all this time.'

'Better late than never,' she laughed, not entirely sure she wanted to identify the feelings churning through her. 'Fancy a fight?'

'I don't mean anything, I'm just checking,' Andy shrugged now, as Jade refilled her water bottle. He moved closer and Jade fought against the impulse to shrink back. 'I just want to make sure you're okay.'

'You know I'm right, by the way?' Jade blurted.

'What?'

'When I come to your flat. I get upset because it seems to me that you've moved in with her a couple of days after we split up.'

'Yeah, because you get confused.'

'But how old's your baby? Five, six months? So you must have been with her within weeks of our split. I might get the details wrong, but I'm right about that, for what it's worth.'

'Come on Jade, don't start —'

Jade held up her hands with a grin. 'I'm not starting anything. I'm just saying.'

'Well what's the point? It's all in the past now.'

'There's no point, Andy. No point at all.'

'Jade hold on —'

But Jade turned and walked across the mats towards the changing rooms, glee fizzing through her. She hadn't even realised until that moment that part of what upset her about the episodes was the idea that she had meant so little to Andy he had moved on without a second thought. But he had and that didn't kill her, she thought with a grin, firmly deciding that a wee celebratory cartwheel of joy would be overkill.

CARA CURLED up in the battered old armchair in her spare room and read the file that Ruari had given her. It was a detailed log of everything he had done over the past eighteen months since she hired him to find Stellan. There was a steady rat-a-tat of rain against the window, and even in daylight the small lamp she'd put on didn't banish the shadows from the room. Cara pulled the duvet from the spare bed over her knees as she read.

Ruari was diligent, she thought, marvelling at his copious, detailed notes. She had tasked him with finding the needle of one person in the haystack of the entire world, and he had tackled it like a dog with a bone, scouring the internet for potential sightings, compiling lists of empty properties the length and breadth of Scotland and systematically working through each one. He had even created a profile of Stellan, quizzing her, his yoga crew and rock climbing buddies, as well as several old friends and relatives in Sweden. He had listed Stellan's interests, his qualities and habits, and brainstormed ways they could potentially reveal his whereabouts.

Cara looked up from the file a moment, feeling overwhelmed. She noticed that the tea she had brought up with her was stone cold, and glanced out at the unrelenting rain. She was horribly conscious that if she had bothered to put her Fitbit on that morning, it would register about seventeen steps. The thought crossed her mind that if she and Stellan had ever got around to getting the dog they'd discussed for years, she would have been forced out for a walk even in this rain.

She'd never thought to mention that to Ruari, she thought with a smile, then a chill washed over her as she realised that was it.

Years ago, not long after they met, she and Stellan had gone on a walking holiday in the far north of Sweden. One day as they trekked through Abisko National Park, keeping their eyes peeled for wild reindeer, they'd blethered their usual nonsense, covering, amongst other subjects, childhood stories, weirdest dreams and the fact that neither of them was certain whether or not they'd ever tried key lime pie.

At one point Cara had said something about how she thought Stellan had the spirit of a Labrador because he was so enthusiastic and open and generous with his emotions. He'd replied that she was more of a Collie, sharp and determined and more than a little bit bonkers. They'd gone into fits of laughter and made a solemn vow that if they ever lost one another they would get a dog so they would still be together in spirit.

It was completely daft and Cara had forgotten all about it, but in that moment she was certain that wherever he was, Stellan had a dog. She pulled up a search of every shelter in Scotland and picked up her phone to ring the first one.

· · ·

RUARI HALF-WATCHED the American drama that Hannah was
addicted to and he pretended he just liked for the music.
She'd offered to watch the latest episode on her iPad in the
bedroom as he was working, but he mock reluctantly told
her to fire it upon the TV, promising he could put his
earphones on if he got too distracted. She curled up on the
sofa with her head in his lap, as beautiful Americans back-
stabbed and fell in love. Ruari absentmindedly played with
her hair as he scrolled through his laptop screen with the
other hand.

It was mindless work. He wasn't entirely sure what he
was looking for as he combed through the dozens and
dozens of chat forums about death row and celebrity death
row prisoners. It had just been a hunch that he might pick
up something about Stuart Henderson that would blossom
into a line of inquiry, that would help him confirm or deny
Amy's mad theory.

He suspected she had been a bit stung by his refusal to
believe her. He had snapped more than he meant to, he
remembered uncomfortably, but he'd taken Amy's word
without question before and it had ended up with Greer in
prison. He knew that wasn't entirely fair, but he felt respon-
sible for it all spiralling out of control.

He should have gone directly to the police with what
Amy had told him that long ago night in the coffee shop off
Dumbarton Road. Maybe, somehow, McAvoy would have
been stopped sooner. Maybe he would have been arrested
without Greer's life being destroyed. Maybe Ruari would
have been able to consider the police desk job Cara had
suggested once upon a time. It wasn't Amy's fault, it was
Ruari's, he thought, as Hannah caught his hand and pulled
it to her face to kiss the palm.

'You're tense,' she muttered. 'You okay?'

'These forums are depressing.'

So far he had mostly come across heartbreaking posts from families of victims pleading as to why the monster who took their sister or daughter was still alive and well at tax payers' expense, and a handful of disturbing threads in which women planned weddings to prisoners. He had just clicked away from a miserable account of a woman detailing her attempts to get her wedding dress finished before her intended's execution date, when his was eye caught by a folder of threads marked *the Four Percent*.

Something about that rang a bell. Someone had once told him about how it's estimated that 4% of death row prisoners are innocent, and that the name had been taken by a group dedicated to overturning convictions. He could picture having the conversation, remembered nodding in horror. The conversation must have been related to Stuart somehow, he thought, though he was fairly sure it wasn't Amy he was thinking of. Greer? Maybe.

'How can they know who is innocent?' Hannah asked. She sat up and paused the TV.

'Looks like it was started by a group of law students.' Ruari frowned, skimming through the website he had found linked to in the forum. 'They were assigned death row cases for mock trials in their final year of law school, and while investigating, two of them — out of a class of thirty-six — came across evidence proving the defendant's innocence. They managed to mount successful appeals in both cases, and that's when they started this group. It looks as though officially it is a legal advocacy group, reinvestigating cases and filing appeals if or when they find something.'

'What do you mean officially?'

'Well there is a post here from a woman thanking them for, quote 'giving her the love of her life back.' Someone's replied asking if she means they overturned a conviction. Her next post is asking why she can't delete or edit her original post, and she sounds stressed. Then,' Ruari scrolled some more, his eyes widening as he read. 'There's a link here to another thread where they're discussing the rumours that if this group can't legally secure the release of a prisoner they believe to be innocent, they get them out of prison. They think that's what the woman meant, that they literally got her husband back.'

'What do you mean, 'get them out of prison?' You can't just get folk out of prison. Especially not death row. How could that be possible?'

Ruari shrugged. 'I don't have a clue,' he said. He kept scrolling, trying to ignore the horrifying possibility that this could mean Amy was right.

Then his eye caught something and his blood turned to lead. 'What's the matter?' Hannah asked softly. Ruari hadn't even realised he had muttered *no* out loud.

Rättfärdighet.

It was a user name that popped up throughout the forum. The user passionately and articulately argued through several threads against the death penalty even when the accused was guilty. He — or she — advocated for the abolishment of capital punishment worldwide and for all death row prisoners to be freed on humanitarian grounds.

'Can you look that word up on your phone?' Ruari asked Hannah, knowing what she would say before she did.

'It means justice or righteousness,' she said softly. He looked up and met her heartsick gaze. 'In Swedish.'

That was when Ruari remembered. It had been Stellan who told him about the Four Percent group.

. . .

KEVIN'S KNOCK was answered by a harassed looking woman with long blond hair. She started to shake her head even before he got a chance to speak.

'No, I'm sorry. I don't know if you're a charity mugger or what, but I give everything I can afford already and I've got a teething baby in here so I really don't have time for whatever you're after. Sorry.'

There was a baby mewling irritably from somewhere inside the flat, but Kevin held up his ID before she could close the door. 'I'm police,' he said with an apologetic smile. 'I'm sorry to disturb you and I won't take any much of yer time, I promise. It's actually your partner I wanted to speak tp, if he's home?'

'He's not,' she said with a tight smile.

'I've tried the mobile number I had for him, but it's dead. Could I maybe take his new number?'

The woman shook her head, then burst into tears. 'Sorry,' she muttered.

'No bother at all. Look I can come back another time, or I can make you a nice cup of tea and then come back another time? I just need a wee word with him, but it's probably nothing.'

'I don't know where he is,' the woman gasped through her sobs as the baby's cries got louder. 'He just — we had a fight, a week ago, and he stormed out. I thought he was just going to cool off, but he's not been back since and his mobile stopped working.'

'How long after he walked out did his mobile stop working?'

'I'm not sure. I was angry, and I thought the baby had a temperature, so I didn't even try to phone him till that evening. What would it be, six hours later? It went to that dead tone already.'

'Have you been in touch with his friends, family?'

She gave a bitter smile. 'There's not really anybody. He fell out with his mum and dad when he was a teenager and left home, I just met them once when they came to visit me in hospital when I had the baby. He threw them out and I've not seen them since. And he's never really had any pals since I've known him. He used to play on a five-a-side team and drank with them from time to time, but he gave that up a while ago and I got the impression they were quite happy to see the back of him.'

She gave a helpless shrug and folded her arms as though trying to get warm. 'Andy's a difficult character,' she said quietly. 'I'm worried about him, but — I'm also not sure I want him to come back.'

'YEAH, one of the guys cracked pretty easily,' Cody said.

Ruari starstruck when the woman who had streamed Stuart Henderson's press conference live to the world answered his call. Cody had teased in an Instagram story that she was about to break something huge on Stuart Henderson pretty soon. Ruari took a chance and messaged her, and she replied within moments to set up a call.

'Seems like something almost went wrong on the last bust they did and he's spooked.' She laughed. 'He told me he would talk to me in exchange for immunity. I'm like, sure dude, I can definitely promise you I will never arrest you.'

'I thought they were law students?'

'The core group is, as far as I've figured so far, but they bring in carefully vetted folks to help on the busts. He told me he was brought in because he'd done a stretch at the prison and knew the layout pretty well from the inside, but you know what I think? I think they bring in the extra person to be the patsy. I think he was there to be the one to get caught if anybody was, which lets the Four Percenters melt into the background. He cracked too easy to really be one of them.'

'So he won't know anything useful to us then, will he?' said Ruari.

'Oh my god I'm sorry, but I just have to say how much I love your accent,' Cody said suddenly. 'I never heard one in real life. Could you just say 'freedom', like one time?'

'Umm, freedom,' muttered Ruari awkwardly.

'That's the most amazing thing I ever heard. I wish I had an accent.'

Ruari nodded, thinking that someone should break it to her she had an American accent. 'Anyway, the guy?'

'Right, no. He's definitely not inner sanctum or anything, but with the other digging I did around Henderson, I feel like a picture is emerging. The prison governor totally blew me off, by the way, I could have cried. I got nothing even when I challenged him about the meals. He's good, but then to keep something like this quiet for two years? He'd have to be. My theory is he knows but he turns a blind eye for some reason. I don't know why yet, I'm thinking debt, blackmail? I'm working on it.'

'Does this group actually think Stuart Henderson is innocent?' asked Ruari. 'Even Amy doesn't believe that.'

'They believe the prosecution didn't prove his guilt beyond a reasonable doubt, and that's their thing. I mean, that's the core of our justice system, right? I don't know what it's like in Scotland, but here nobody has to *prove* anybody innocent. The burden of proof is with the State to prove guilt -- and when it's a capital case it needs to be beyond a shadow of a doubt. The group seem to believe that without Henderson's confessions the case against him was weak.'

'Who in their right mind would confess to those murders if they didn't do them?'

'I guess, but it's less about his actual innocence than whether the Constitutional requirements for capital punishment are met. The group's ultimate aim is to abolish the death penalty, so the more they can find cases that prove it's been applied inconsistently or whatever, the better. They think Henderson's trial was rushed to get the guilty verdict people were demanding, like some kind of medieval blood lust, and that too much of the evidence was circumstantial.

'Henderson was placed in the towns where the murders he was tried for took place, he definitely talked to some of the victims, and in once case danced with one of the them in a bar, but in terms of indisputable evidence he committed all those murders? They didn't have enough for when somebody's life is at stake.'

'But isn't Henderson a millionaire? Surely he could afford the best lawyers out there?'

'Right, but according to the Four Percent, that was actually part of the problem. There was all this hype about this, like, legal Dream Team but they were all for show. I went back and watched every second of the trial and read some transcripts, and to be honest, I kind of agree. They were grandstanding, making a show of the whole thing with an eye on publishing deals and running for office — which, by the way, three out of four of them have now done — instead of actually defending their client.

'Like I said, maybe he did the murders, but he did not get the standard of defence that the whole justice system rests on. And I mean, it fails a rich white dude? What chance does literally anybody else have? The second trial, the death penalty trial, was a little more circumspect —'

'What do you mean?'

'Okay, so two trials have to take place before the death penalty is applied. The first one determines whether or not the defendant is guilty, and if they are, a second trial is immediately held to decide whether the Constitutional requirements for capital punishment have been met. They're often considered one by the media because they follow back-to-back — and actually I didn't even know until I started researching all this — but legally, they are two separate entities.

'Once Henderson had been found guilty on the nineteen counts of murder they charged him with, the media and everybody pretty much considered the death penalty a done deal and so all the hype died down, and right away the so-called Dream Team quit. He actually had a public defender, this, like, hairless kid in short pants right out of law school defending him against a lethal injection. Even if he's guilty, I've gotta say I don't think that's right.'

'So they broke him out of prison?'

'Well the kid I talked to can't say that for sure, he wasn't involved if they did. But he does know this — another kid, sounds to me like somebody else at his level — was sent to the UK Embassy to pick up a British passport — like a replacement, if it was lost or stolen, right? — right around the time Henderson disappeared. Oh — and speaking of foreign people? The Swedish username you asked about — I did some digging, and it seems like a lot of folks on the forums are pretty sure this guy is police. Mostly because of jargon, or whatever, that he used.'

Ruari nodded. 'That would make sense if it is the person I'm afraid it is,' he sighed. 'His wife is a senior detective.'

'Right, so he could have picked up shop talk from her. Sorry if it is this guy, dude.'

'If it helps us find him then it's a good thing. I hope.'

'I'm sure you probably have your own questionable dark internet contact already, but my guy is the best, if it helps. No matter what somebody did to reroute their IP address, he'll be able to find out where they really are — or at least where they were, when they posted. I can put you in touch?'

'That would be great, thanks.'

'Okay, I have to go right now, but is there anything else?'

'The British passport — did your guy know what name it was in?'

'Shit, right, of course. I wrote it down... here it is. Charlie MacGregor. Cool name, huh?'

'You can change your mind at any moment,' said Amy, and Jade nodded. A shiver wracked through her.

They were standing outside the Indian takeaway where Jade had cried into the maitre'd's mum's hair the night Andy left her. Amy was holding the keys to the van she had rented that afternoon. Jade was wearing the scratchy monstrosity.

That was why she kept finding it.

She's put it on that night, so she could smell Andy while she cried her eyes out, and it had ended up saving her from hypothermia while she tramped through the Campsies. It was never really Andy's jumper, she realised now. It was always her Gran's.

'Let's do it,' she said, giving Amy a grin she knew didn't fool her for a second. 'Before I chicken out.'

E ven in first gear, Cara's car struggled with the steep dirt track. It whined and slid and span, and eventually Cara reversed back down to the layby on the main road behind and got out to walk.

There was a filthy white van parked haphazardly by the side of the road which looked as though it had been abandoned yonks ago. Cara pulled her car around behind the van so it wouldn't immediately be seen. She had no idea what time it was when she had made her 78th call to an animal shelter and a woman with a deep smoker's voice immediately recognised Stellan's description.

'Oh aye, he wore one of those hoodies my grandsons are into, so I never saw him properly, but I ken just who you mean. I suspected he was maybe living rough, but him and Maisie fell right in love with each other, so they did. I decided they would do each other good and I let him away with her. This was, what, a year and a half ago, give or take?'

'Right,' said Cara, her heart sinking. 'I suppose you wouldn't have any clue where he is now.'

'Aye,' the woman said. Cara could hear the smile in her voice. 'They're back. Saw no sign of them for well over a year, but I spotted Maisie the other day waiting outside the wee corner shop, and my grandsons saw her up at the bothy the other day. I've not actually laid eyes on your man, but I suspect wherever Maisie is, he is. Could have moved on by now, I suppose, but there was smoke coming from the bothy last night.'

'The bothy? Have you got an address?'

The woman laughed. 'It's not got an address, hen. But if you come up here I'll point you in the right direction. It's not easy to get to, mind. That's how it's normally empty.'

It was now full dark and raining as Cara scrabbled her way carefully upwards, remembering Stellan's advice from when they tackled Ben Nevis a few summers ago. She could almost hear his voice in her mind: *just keep a steady pace and trust your body to find its balance.* The only sound was the soft pitter-patter of rain on leaves, no animals scuttled or birds shrieked. Cara's hands were grazed and her jeans sodden with mud by the time she reached a spot flat enough to stand. The bothy was in darkness.

The moon came out from behind a cloud and she saw that there were two narrow slits of windows facing her. They looked like dead eyes watching her. Cara hesitated, then began to approach slowly. Her footsteps made no sound on the soft, wet, grass, but she suspected the ground might turn to gravel the closer she got.

The cottage was above the tree line, but it was tucked into a sharp ridge. She scuttled lightly to the ridge, felt its mossy outline. She was at the side of the cottage now, out of sight of the windows. If she approached this way, she was confident anyone inside the cottage could not be sure where she was.

She heard something and froze. An owl hooted some-where in the distance. Cara rolled her eyes at herself and took another step forwards when she heard the creak. The door. It was opening. Her heart pounded, blood roared in her ears. There was nowhere to hide. In the pitch blackness she maybe had a chance of escape, but she knew already that she wasn't going anywhere if Stellan was there. Let him take them both.

Another noise, that she couldn't quite identify. She sank to a crouch, grateful for her black jumper, peering intently into the darkness, her every cell on alert. She heard it again. Breathing. Thick breathing, snuffly. Someone with a cold? Then a wet nose was pushed into her face, a happy tail flapped rain over her.

'Maisie, I presume?' she whispered.

Just then she heard the roar of a rattly engine starting up, a screech of jamming gears. The white van. Cara ran from the ridge and raced back down as fast as she dared without breaking her neck, but when she reached the road the van was long gone.

'Damnit —' she howled hopelessly into the wind, wanting to lie down in the road and scream. She stared frantically up and down the silent, dark road, but there was no way to tell which way the van had gone. Maisie pawed at her with a whine, and Cara reached down to stroke her head while she wracked her brains as to what to do next. It hadn't crossed her mind to take the van's license plate number, she thought in frustration. She'd barely noticed it. She had been too focussed on Stellan.

There was something tucked into Maisie's collar. A flimsy wire bound notebook. Cara stared at it, then ran to the car. Maisie hopped in ahead of her and sat eagerly in the passenger seat, thumping her tail against the leather. Cara put the light on and paged in wonder through months and months of Stellan's tiny, neat, handwriting, a lump forming in her throat.

She thumbed carefully to the last page and saw *he wants to go to where Ruari's friend was murdered. I am afraid.*

Lorna, Cara thought. The fallen tree near Lennoxtown. She wiped the tears from her cheeks with the back of her hand as she turned the ignition and clicked her fingers for Maisie to jump into the backseat. She didn't have time to cry now. She could melt down once she had found Stellan.

THE RAIN WAS steady as Jade and Amy hiked silently in the darkness. The orange glow of Glasgow hovered on the horizon far below, the clouds were low and brooding in the deep purple sky. Amy lost too much peripheral vision with her hood up, so she had shoved it down when they'd first started to climb from the carpark. Her hair was soaking and rain streaked across her face, dripping from her nose.

Jade didn't even have a coat. That horrible wiry jumper was sodden. It had to be weighing her down, but Jade hiked evenly, showing no signs of slowing down.

'Watch out for sheep,' Jade muttered as they rounded a bend. 'They're right crabbit fuckers.'

Amy nodded, though she knew Jade couldn't see her. An icy, dark feeling was slithering through her as she recognised where they were, where they were going. She couldn't think about it, not yet. She had to be here for Jade. But as they broke the treeline and she spied the crumbling wall in the distance, she had to grit her teeth to keep her breathing even.

'I felt woozy when we walked along here,' Jade was

saying. 'He gripped my arm like a vice so I couldn't fall, could do nothing but walk where he pointed me. That's right,' she nodded. 'I had a bruise there, the next day. I didn't know why.'

'What kind of woozy?'

Not dizzy, exactly, more — I kept thinking I was dreaming, and then I'd trip or stub my toe and come-to for a second, then slip back into this daze thing. I felt sort of, numb and queasy.'

Chloroform, thought Amy. It was Amy herself who had told Stuart about its history as an anaesthetic and use as a sedative after reading about it for one of her classes.

Unless you were a baddie in a film, it was fairly difficult to knock someone out cold with chloroform outside of a medical setting, but repeated small doses could produce a woozy, even trance-like state. The only time Amy had cried in front of the FBI was when they told her that minute traces of chloroform had been found in two of his victim's bloodstreams. *I did that,* she had thought.

They rounded the final bend and the moon came out from behind a cloud. Amy could clearly see the outline of the collapsed tree Lorna Stewart had murdered with rotten eggs once upon a time.

'He laughed when he saw that tree,' Jade said, her voice tight and strained.

An icy gust of wind splattered rain against them. Amy could see the tragic wee tree swaying dangerously. 'This weird, high, laugh like a hyena or something.'

'Yeah he always does that,' she whispered.

'I appreciate your time,' Ruari said into the webcam. The

room on the other side was in semi darkness, though he was fairly sure it was still daytime in the States. He could only just make out the enormous man who sat in front of the camera, surrounded by monitors.

'Don't thank me, just pay me,' Cody's IT contact wheezed. He had introduced himself only as mdx32.

'It should be in your account already,' Ruari said, wondering if he would manage his half of the rent after the staggering amount had all but cleaned him out. Cara would cover it, he knew, but he felt guilty not clearing such an expense with her in advance.

'Yeah, I see it.'

Mdx32 fell silent a moment, frowning at the screen. The only sounds were the click of his mouse, the whirr of a computer fan somewhere in the background, and his laboured breathing. Impatience churned through Ruari, but he sensed that hurrying mdx32 would result in the call being cut off, money or no money.

'Alright,' mxd32 said finally. 'So I thought this was the zip code, but it has letters in it, so I don't know what —'

'That's a British zip code,' Ruari said quickly.

'Oh right, okay cool. So — you got a pen? Cool. It's G61—'

Ruari's heart fell as he scribbled the address mxd32 gave him. G61. Bearsden -- where Stellan and Cara lived. Stellan had been communicating with the people who would break Stuart Henderson out of prison from the home he shared with Cara.

CARA TOUCHED the brakes as she rounded a corner, ruefully remembering how she'd tried to argue with Stellan that they didn't really need a powerful Saab designed for tackling the Arctic Circle to cut about the West End of Glasgow. She was grateful now: the car had taken narrow bends on the winding road at seventy, eighty miles an hour in its stride.

She had caught up to the white van within minutes.

She had a blue light in the glove box, but suspected whoever was driving wouldn't respond to being pulled over, and if she slowed down to signal to them she could risk losing them. She had considered running the van off the road, confident that her car would easily get the better of the rickety van that bounced and swerved wildly around bends, but she was afraid of hurting Stellan.

They had to know she was following them. They were in the middle of nowhere. In well over an hour they hadn't passed a single other car, it felt as though the entire world had narrowed to just their two vehicles speeding dangerously through the Trossachs. Maisie was lying on the back seat, whining softly. Every once in a while Cara heard her tail thump and felt as though she were quietly cheering her on.

'I won't lose them, girl,' she muttered as Maisie popped her head up. 'Don't you worry about that.'

A sign for Aberfoyle had flashed by minutes before, soon they would zip over the main road that went to Stirling, then through a series of wee villages as they approached the Campsies.

Cara fumbled in the glove compartment for the blue light, expertly steering the car with one hand as she opened the driver's window. They were sure to encounter a car or two soon. Even if it risked alerting the van, she needed to warn passersby.

They had turned towards the Campsies at Strathblane by the time she got the siren on, and she saw the van ahead leap forwards in a burst of speed and veered dangerously onto the verge. Cara's heart was in her mouth as its seemed for a moment as though it would smash into the high hedge, but at the last second the driver righted it, and it sped on.

Cara drew up a mental map of the area she knew like the back of her hand. To get to the carpark she was sure the van was headed to, you had to go right into Lennoxtown then double back. If she turned off before then, there wasn't another road, but wasn't there a track, somewhere behind the wee tea room maybe, that the car might just get far enough up to be able to head them off? Even if she had to leave the car, she might just make it through the woods to that crooked tree before them.

It meant losing sight of the van, she thought desperately. What if her following had spooked them and they'd decided not to head for Lorna's death-site after all? The turn off for Clachan of Campsie approached and she made a split second decision, swung the car left with a controlled skid and a spray of gravel, praying that she wasn't giving up her last glimpse of Stellan.

RUARI PEDALLED FURIOUSLY through the quiet grounds of Gartnavel Hospital. He'd tried phoning Cara several times, but her phone went straight to voicemail, so finally he grabbed his bike. She needed to know as soon as possible, he thought, his mind racing as to what on earth Stellan's involvement in the Four Percent could mean.

Even if Stellan somehow believed in Henderson's innocence, he wouldn't have voluntarily left Cara to — what? Help him? Babysit him all this time?

Ruari was breathing heavily by the time he pulled up outside Cara's gates. The house was shrouded in darkness, the driveway empty. He stared at it in confusion as he tried to get his breath back. Where would she have gone at this time of night in the midst of everything? He would wait, he decided. Wherever she was, she would come home sooner or later.

As Ruari hopped off his bike and prepared to set up camp on the pavement, something occurred to him and he fumbled in his pocket for the address he had written down. He had never before paid any attention to Cara's address: the first time he had gone there, Cara had driven -- and thereafter he had just followed the same route without noticing street names. Now though, it occurred to him that the address hadn't rung a bell at all.

He stared at the note he had scribbled, then jogged to the end of Cara's cul-de-sac to check the sign. It wasn't the same. Ruari pulled out his phone and typed the address into his map app. It was less than a mile away. He grabbed his bike and pulled out onto the main road.

'THERE WERE TWO OF THEM,' Jade whispered. Amy wanted to take her hand, but she was afraid of disturbing her recollection. She stayed a few feet away, by the wall, as Jade slowly turned around, her eyes wide as though she were watching a replay of that night.

'That's what — that's what felt wrong, when I thought I had remembered what he looked like. It wasn't him. The blond guy didn't drive, he didn't attack me. I think he stopped him. He saved me. That's why the killer didn't come after me when I hit him with my bag and got over the wall. I glanced back and I caught sight of the blond guy, but he wasn't chasing me. He was — he was holding him back. He was letting me escape.'

The rain had stopped and the night was still, silently waiting.

'It was Stuart, wasn't it? Your husband, who attacked me.'

Amy nodded. The moon came out from behind a cloud and bathed them in a silvery glow. The crooked tree was silhouetted against the purple sky. Though terror was prickling over Amy, she couldn't help but smile. It felt as though Lorna were there, cheering them on.

Fuckin' grab him by the baws and TWIST. Give him a wee black eye for good measure, with my compliments.

'Why didn't he ever come after me again?' Jade said. 'He must have known I would remember eventually.'

'Because we made a deal,' said a soft voice and Amy whirled around in fright.

'Stellan —' The word caught in her throat as she realised he wasn't alone.

'He had me in the back of the van already when he picked you up. After you were both gone, I managed to get the door open.'

'You could have escaped.'

'I knew what he was going to do to you. I caught up just as you hit him with your bag. He was stunned, you would have got away anyway I think, but we made a deal. I promised him that I would stay with him as long as he did not kill anyone.'

'I ken that *gentleman* isnae the first word folk think of when they think of' me,' said Stuart Henderson, and Amy's heart leapt into her mouth. The familiarity of his voice washed over her and tears sprang into her eyes. For a mad moment, she thought she would turn and run into his arms. 'But I am a man of my word.'

Amy noticed that Stuart had stepped onto a rock which made him almost Stellan's height. He loomed above her, silhouetted by the moon, and Amy felt a sudden, chilling sense of what he had looked like to his victims. A wind blew up and the crooked tree creaked. Amy thought it was Lorna laughing. *Man of his word, my bum.*

'Why did you need Stellan to stay with you?' she asked, and Stuart shrugged.

'Ach I thought he could teach me to talk to Henrik Larsson,' he grinned.

'Was it to get to Cara?'

It was a waste of time: Stuart would never answer a direct question, Amy thought in frustration. She had a maddening sense of time running out. It was so surreal seeing Stuart in the flesh after all these years, a part of her half expected him to disappear in a puff of blue smoke. 'What has Cara got to do with you?'

'Why me?' Jade demanded.

'Because you were sad,' Stuart said softly. 'You were walking along the road greetin' like your wee heart would break and I couldnae stand it. That's what the FBI never worked out. Every lassie I took, she had such sadness comin' from her it pure broke my heart. They all wanted put out their misery, that's the truth of it. I was like — I was like an Angel of Mercy. I would've put you out yours if this great stoater haudnae stopped me.'

'What a load of shite, Stuart,' Amy snapped.

Stuart giggled. 'Aye right enough,' he chuckled. 'Oh Amy-girl, I've missed you. I just fuckin' kill anybody that catches my eye. I could've picked the lassie in front o' you or behind you,' he shrugged to Jade. 'I don't give a midge on a monkey's bum who it is. It's just the luck of the draw. I don't hate anybody, I just like killing.'

He threw back his head and howled into the wind and Amy couldn't decide whether he looked terrifyingly savage or daft as a brush.

'Mind, Amy, when all the papers in America were calling me a sexist and all that shite?' he demanded. 'I was pure offended. I'm nothing of the kind, I think lassies are brilliant — present company being my one and only numero uno, of course.' His voice took on an injured, whiny tone and Amy wanted to nut him. He held his hands up in surrender. 'Ken why I don't kill men? Cause I'm a wee guy and they're all bigger than me.'

'That's a pish and all,' Amy spat, fury churning in her. 'Stellan, he's been lying to you.'

'No,' breathed Stellan in horror. 'Stuart — no.'

'No I havnae,' shouted Stuart, stamping his foot. 'You take that back.'

'Stuart has murdered at least two men in the past week and left their bodies out for me.'

'Do you think I'm a FUCKIN' CAT?' Stuart roared. 'Fuckin' leavin' dead bodies about the place for you? What kind of nutcase would do that? I've been leaving you SOCKS. Fucks sake, Amy.'

'Is that why we came close to Glasgow, Stuart?' Stellan asked.

Quick as lightning, Stuart leapt across the boggy grass and grabbed hold of Jade, nimbly trapping her windpipe in the crook of his elbow. 'If yous are gonnae have such a low opinion of me, then why exactly I'm I fuckin' behaving?

'Two years I've put up with your shite love and laughter patter, you big stupid Viking, and you fuckin' believe my wee wife ower me? Cheers very much, pal.'

As Amy and Stellan leapt forward, Stuart squeezed and Jade's knees buckled.

RUARI PULLED up at the second set of gates and stared at the house. It was a detached sandstone mansion set back from the road, almost identical to Cara's.

For a second, Ruari wondered if he'd just ridden round the block and ended up right back where he started in some mad horror film dream where you keep opening the front door to find yourself back where you started. But as he sat on his bike, wondering what to do next, he spied a set of headlights turning into the road, He instinctively rode on a few metres until the car turned into the driveway he had just left.

He leaned his bike against the wall of the next door neighbour's house and crept back, peering carefully round the stone gate post as the powerful BMW crunched up the gravel. There were two people in the car. As he watched, the house security lights came on, bathing the driveway in light, and the driver and passenger doors opened. Ruari reached for his phone and swiped to open the camera, took a never ending burst of photos as he watched Detective Superintendent Liam Kavanagh jog up the steps to his front door, jangling the keys in his hand.

He unlocked the door, chatting easily with the other man. Ruari heard a burst of laughter as the other man patted his pockets then gestured to the car. He turned to head back to the car for whatever he had forgotten, and Ruari caught sight of his face.

Once Ruari saw a face, he never forgot it. He remembered Hannah's grimace as she pointed to that face on a Facebook photo of her, Jade and a group of friends from a

Hogmanay party a few years before. Ruari had laughed when Hannah muttered darkly about photoshopping him out, said he still had photos of Aoife about the place, that it wasn't healthy to completely erase an ex's existence.

'Aye, but you don't know what a weapon this one was,' she'd muttered and deleted the photo.

As Ruari watched, Jade's ex-boyfriend Andy grabbed his phone from Liam's car then headed inside the house. Liam shut the door behind them.

AMY SCREAMED as Jade sank to the ground.

Maisie leapt out of the darkness and bit Stuart on the bum. He howled with pain as Maisie sank her teeth into his arse and Jade slipped out of his grip, whirled around and kneed him in the balls. Stuart fell to his knees and Jade staggered, trembling, into Amy's arms.

'You're okay, he can't hurt you now. It's all over,' Amy muttered through chattering teeth, staring at Stuart crumpled in the mud.

'Cara!' screamed Stellan, hurtling down the hill to meet her as she emerged from the woods.

Amy led Jade out of Stuart's reach, fumbled for her phone though she knew that there was rarely any service up where they were. She should restrain Stuart somehow, she knew. Sit on him or something, but she couldn't bring herself to go any nearer. He was curled up like a baby on the mud, moaning. Amy was holding Jade, though she wasn't sure whether it was for Jade's comfort or her own.

'I called for backup before I left the car,' Cara gasped through sobs of relief as she and Stellan approached, their arms wrapped around one another. 'They won't be long.'

Maisie yipped, and Jade wriggled out of Amy's arms.

'The fucker is getting away,' she yelled. She, Cara and Stellan took off after Stuart's retreating figure. Amy was frozen, a great flood of icy fear crashing over her as she clutched onto the wall, her breath coming in short, sharp gasps. Somewhere in the distance sirens approached as she heard Stuart's scream echo through the still night.

END EPISODE FIVE

ALSO BY C.S DUFFY

Thank you so much for reading Dark of Night: Episode Five - I really hope you enjoyed it!! And if you're dying to find out whether they catch up with Stuart, fear not because the SERIES FINALE is released on 10 January, 2019!

Dark of Night: Episode Five

As you may know, reviews are precious to authors, so if you are enjoying the *Dark of Night* series, I would be so grateful if you could pop on Amazon and let the world know what you think!

Also, there is a Facebook group for those who have read *Dark of Night*... imaginatively called **I've Read Dark of Night**! Pop over there for all sorts of chat and chances to win advance copies of future books!

Thanks again!

Claire xx